WINNER OF THE 33RD ANNUAL INTERNATIONAL
3-DAY NOVEL CONTEST

YAK!

JENNIFER K. CHUNG

WINNER OF THE 33RD ANNUAL INTERNATIONAL 3-DAY NOVEL CONTEST

3-DAY BOOKS

VANCOUVER • TORONTO

Terroryaki!
Copyright © 2011
by Jennifer K. Chung

All rights reserved. No part of this
book may be reproduced by any
means without the prior permission
of the publisher, with the exception
of brief passages in reviews.

EDITED BY Kris Rothstein
DESIGN AND ILLUSTRATIONS
BY Mauve Pagé

Library and Archives Canada Cataloguing
in Publication

Chung, Jennifer K., 1979-
    Terroryaki! / Jennifer K. Chung.

ISBN 978-1-55152-412-2

    I. Title.

PS3603.H845T47 2011
    813'.6   C2011-903973-7

Distributed in Canada by University of
Toronto Press and in the United States
by Consortium through Arsenal Pulp
Press (www.arsenalpulp.com).

This is a work of fiction. Any
resemblance to persons either living
or deceased is purely coincidental.

PUBLISHED BY:
3-Day Books
PO Box 2106, Station Terminal
Vancouver, BC V6B 3T5, Canada

info@3daynovel.com
www.3daynovel.com

The text of this book is printed on
100% post-consumer recycled paper.

Printed in Canada.

For Mom, Dad, and Erica

I

SAMANTHA WAS GETting married, and Mom didn't like it. She thought Sam's fiancé was a bad match for her and predicted that Sam would be divorced within a year. I kinda liked the guy—Patrick often joined me on weekly expeditions to new restaurants—but Mom didn't care about my opinion. Patrick wasn't Asian enough for her, probably because he wasn't Asian at all. Besides, Mom and Sam have had a rocky relationship ever since Sam went away to college, and Mom was always bugging me about Sam, asking if I'd talked to her or if she'd posted on Facebook. I always shrugged and said, "I dunno."

We were coming up toward the wedding, and Sam was flying back from the East Coast for an early bridal shower. Because I still lived at home with our parents, I'd arranged the entire thing and sent all the invites—Sunday afternoon tea at a cousin's house in Green Lake. The weather forecast predicted a beautiful Seattle summer day, and I was looking forward to seeing all of our friends and family.

Sam usually stayed with Patrick when she was in town, so I was surprised to hear her ringtone on Friday night.

"What's up?"

"Daisy, I need you to pick me up. I'm at the airport."

"I thought Patrick was supposed to pick you up."

"He's busy." Sometimes, her voice could freeze the sun.

"I'll see you in thirty minutes."

The wait took the edge off my sister, but she still looked pissed; her aura announced her prickly mood, and even the smokers walked the extra twenty feet to the Designated Smoking Area to avoid Sam's five feet and seven inches of righteous, pony-tailed fury. I popped the trunk of my dark blue Honda Civic. It's about six years old and nothing special except for the cute zombie sock monkey on the dash-board, an artifact from my brief sewing phase. I called him *Braaains*.

"Where am I taking you? Home or Patrick's?"

"What's Mom like tonight?"

"She made beef noodle soup for dinner. She was reheating it for you when I left." It was Sam's favorite dish.

Sam made a face. "I guess we should go home."

I made it all the way to the freeway before she burst: "Boys are so stupid!" Of course it was boys. She was engaged, she was a successful lawyer, she was almost thirty, and it was still all about boys. If my sister were a movie, she'd fail the Bechdel test.

"Where is he, anyway?" I asked, turning down the radio (Queensrÿche, "Take Hold of the Flame").

"San Francisco."

"You told him you were coming back this weekend, right?"

"Patrick is *interviewing*," she spat.

Interesting. One of the defining aspects of the Sam/Patrick relationship was its long-distance nature—Sam practiced law in New York City, and Patrick programmed code at a Seattle-area tech company. Supposedly they'd spent hours discussing this issue, and they'd decided that Sam would move back to Seattle because she had Patrick *and* family here, and Patrick didn't have anything in New York except for Sam. It seemed strange that Patrick would change his mind after all of their negotiations.

"Does your firm have an office in San Francisco?"

"No," she sniffed, picking up Braaains from the dashboard and pulling at his rot-colored limbs. Sometimes I felt like I was the older sister. I adjusted the overhead flap to keep the setting sun out of my eyes.

"Why does he want to move?"

"He hates his job. He says his friend Diego has a startup in San Francisco and they want to hire him. They're developing technology to diverge-converge product lines through synergistic initiatives on the cloud. Diego's offering him a ten percent share in the company. I think it's a terrible idea, but Patrick is stuck on it. He says it's all coming together."

"Oh."

"It's such a bad idea to mix business and friendship. People have litigated so many cases where that stuff went sour."

"That's too bad." It's hard to give Sam advice. It's hit or miss whether she'll thank you and ignore it, or yell at you for presuming to know what it's like to be *her* in *her* situation. Although I liked Patrick, I would've dumped him years ago if it were me. Sometimes he had trouble seeing things from anyone else's point of view, and he often ignored your emails for weeks (worst geek ever, I *swear*). Besides, I preferred tall, dark, and mysterious, and Patrick was short, blond, and blunt. He really *was* a great dining companion, though, despite his ridiculous insistence on using Evite to schedule everything, including lunch for two. (Sam found it "charming.")

Inspired: "Hey Sam, wanna get ice cream?"

"Where?"

"I found this new place online. It's in a strip mall, next to that great Thai place on the Eastside."

"Daisy, that's like saying, 'Meet me at the gas station with the espresso stand.'"

"The one where you always order the tom yum soup with extra shrimp. In Issaquah."

"Oh sure, Eye of the Thaiger."

"Yeah. Yelp says their pistachio ice cream is amazing."

"Sure, we can go." It was hard to give Sam advice, but it was easy to give her distraction.

Sam monologued on the way there, chattering about the law firm interview she had downtown on Monday, about how the other associates at her law firm kept making snide remarks about the Seattle law scene (or lack thereof), about her intimidating matron of a wedding coordinator who often used her clout to put bad vendors out of business. I let her talk without interruption; it was good to fall back into the familiar, comfortable relationship, just me and my older sister. Sam used to drive me around in high school as I fed her hot french fries from the passenger seat, but we hadn't ridden alone in a car together since our great-aunt's funeral six months ago.

"How's school?" Sam finally asked. "Did you pick a major yet?"

"No, I'm still thinking about it."

"Oh, Daisy, you need more direction in your life."

"I know."

"Mom and Dad aren't going to support you forever, you know."

"I know."

"You don't want to flip burgers for the rest of your life, right?"

"Geez, Sam, I know, okay? I'm still thinking about it."

"I'm just trying to help, okay?"

"I don't need your help."

"Whatever, fine." I ignored her. I loved Sam, but she knew where my buttons were.

My achievements (or lack thereof) were a sore point for me, for everyone. It had been difficult to compete with my sister, so I hadn't even tried. I'd cultivated mediocre grades in high school, disappointing teachers who'd remembered the charming, hardworking Sam, who'd swept through the school like a ninja, cutting her legacy into academic records and State honors before you could even blink. I hadn't known what to tell them except, "Sorry."

Compare: Sam scored a perfect 1600 on the old SATs. Daisy scored detention for drawing caricatures on her English tests.

Sam played flute every week during honors band practice. Daisy played hooky every week during piano lessons.

Sam was elegant and stylish, wore her hair shoulder-length with light brown barrettes. Daisy was punk and goth, wore her hair pixie-cut with green-frosted bangs.

Sam completed a J.D. at Columbia Law after four years at Brown. Daisy completed a course at traffic school after four parking violations at Seattle Center. (Wankers.)

Sam was recruited by high-ranking partners to join their law firms. Daisy was recruited by NBC to watch *Law & Order*.

Sam worked at BigLaw in downtown Manhattan, making a six-figure salary. Daisy worked at a small teriyaki joint in the suburbs, making six bucks every half hour.

I'd started taking community college classes two years earlier, after most of my high school friends had already finished their bachelor's degrees. But what I really wanted was to quit school and draw; I loved art in every medium: charcoals and oils and watercolor and pencils, crayons, clay, and tempera paints. I sketched landscapes at dawn and dusk, posted inked manga characters and a sporadic webcomic on my blog, doodled oily designs on the pans at work before destroying them with smiling onion slices and chunks of pink meat. I was happiest with a blank canvas before me and something to fill it with.

I hadn't told my family. My parents wouldn't think art was practical, and Sam couldn't understand any path to success that didn't pass through academia. Besides, I didn't have a concrete plan—just nebulous wants and desires, and that was no way to get family approval. I did make some Google AdSense revenue from my blog, "Teriyaki-do: The Way of Teriyaki," but it certainly wasn't enough.

We pulled into the strip mall and walked over to the ice cream place, a large, well-lit store on the corner of the row, next to a nail salon with spa-like aspirations.

Sam looked up from her Blackberry and broke the silence: "The waffle cone smells pretty good."

"Yeah."

Ice cream thawed the chill in the car, as it often did. Sam ordered a kid's scoop of limoncello sorbet in a cup. I sampled the pistachio and chose cherry-vanilla instead, one large scoop in a fresh waffle cone. We sat outside in the twilight, licking noisily.

"Do you think Patrick is good for me?"

Noncommittal grunt, followed by a slurp.

"We've known each other forever, but we've been long distance for such a long time. I think we're growing apart."

"Mmm."

"It's natural, right? I mean, to worry about this stuff? Right before the wedding?"

"Yeah. You're thinking too much."

"I always do." She sighed. Her smartphone buzzed, and she pulled it out to check the message.

I noticed a dark food truck in the parking lot, on the other side of the strip mall. It had a large logo splashed on one side, but in the ghostly lamplight, I couldn't quite see it.

"Hey," I said.

"What?"

"Can we go check out that food truck?"

Sam looked up and followed the direction of my gaze. "Sure, let's go."

Summer twilight turned to darkness as we walked over with melting ice cream in our cones and cups. When it came to food, Sam was as adventurous as I was, and there was no telling how long the truck would be in town. The suburbs tended to drive them away, or maybe they tended to drive away from the suburbs. Then again, it's not like I was in the habit of visiting Issaquah.

There was no name, only a picture—a wooden boat, wide and shallow, filled with a flat mound of sticky white rice and large pieces of sauce-slathered chicken. The artist had painted a black Skull-and-Chopsticks flag hanging from a jaunty chopstick mast stuck in the rice. Beneath the wooden ship-plate, we read a legend spray-painted in all white caps: THE BEST TERIYAKI IN SEATTLE.

"They're not even in Seattle," I complained.

"Maybe they're on tour. Want to try it?"

"I don't want to get in trouble for spoiling your dinner." But I couldn't ignore the whiff of grilled meat that floated past us in the evening breeze.

"Uh huh. I don't believe you. Let's go."

It was instinct; evolution hadn't bred "fear of sketchy food" into the family DNA, and we'd grown up eating at hole-in-the-wall places with low levels of health inspector approval and high levels of tastiness. It was probably Dad's fault; when Mom complained about sticky tables and dusty floors (and maybe an occasional cockroach), Dad said it was good for our immune systems to eat in different environments. He's an accountant, not a doctor, so I'm not sure he deserved much credibility on this subject, but Mom seemed to buy it.

Sam and I decided to split a small spicy chicken with brown rice. I handed five dollars to a tall, gaunt, long-haired man sporting a short beard and wearing an elaborate black coat ("Goth Teriyaki," I decided). We finished our ice cream while unseen persons prepped our meal in the back of the dark gray truck.

"What number is this?" Sam asked me.

"Seventy-nine." Teriyaki was my particular hobby, and I was always on the hunt for new places, scoping out the competition and looking for ways to improve my technique. I might be a slacker, but I still had pride in my work.

"Anything I should try?"

"Probably not. I have to check the blog. Pat—"

Sam glared.

"I mean, Patrick and I still haven't found anything better than Ducky Teriyaki. Their sauce is perfect."

"Ugh. They're always so slow. I don't know how you guys can stand it."

I gave her a look. "Sam, good teriyaki is always worth waiting for."

"Whatever. I'd rather have fast and tasty than slow and a little tastier."

The strange teriyaki man was watching us, his brow furrowed quizzically. He had a timeless look about him; he could have been anywhere between twenty-five and fifty. I turned to him and asked, "How long have you guys been around?"

"I was serving teriyaki before you were born," he replied in a low, raspy voice, turning his eyes toward me. Definitely Goth Teriyaki.

"I mean, how long have you guys been in Issaquah?"

"We are cursed to move from place to place, luring men to feast upon our wares until we find those who must join our crew, and so release one of us from misery."

His gaze was too intense. I blushed.

"That's cool. Umm, I have to throw this away." I turned and walked to a nearby trash can, slowly wiped the sticky ice cream off my fingers, then tossed the napkins in the bin, stalling. When I came back, Sam was already in full-on lawyer mode. She never could resist an argument.

"If you're so miserable, why don't you leave?" she asked. "It's just a job. You can find another one, even in this economy."

"We are cursed," the man replied gravely.

"But what does that mean? I mean, I need money, too. We all do. It's how we get food and water and shelter, you know, the stuff at the bottom of Maslow's Hierarchy of Needs. That doesn't mean I'm cursed."

"*You* are human. *We* are cursed."

A deep chime rang from inside the truck. The gaunt man retrieved our order and handed a white plastic bag to me. "Enjoy," he said.

"Thanks." By unspoken agreement, we took our purchase back to the car.

"Well, that was weird," Sam said as we split the meal under the bright door light of my Civic.

"Yeah, like, what was up with that guy?"

"I don't know. I still want to know what he meant by 'cursed.'"

"Y'know, this is really good teriyaki. I'm not sure it's the best in Seattle, but it's probably top ten."

"Really? I think it's gross. Want the rest of mine?"

"Sure." I shoveled Sam's chicken onto my half of the take-out box.

"It's too sweet."

"No way. You should try Kawaii Bento if you want too sweet. Trust me, this stuff is good. In my professional opinion, the chicken's just right, the rice is just right, the sauce is just right, and these yellow takuan pickles are awesome on the side. You see how easy the chicken comes apart when you poke it? It's *perfect*."

"Ugh, whatever. I'll save my appetite for Mom's dinner."

"Fine with me." I took a few more bites. "I should get their card or find out if they have a Twitter feed or something. I bet they're kicked out of Issaquah in a week."

"Yeah."

But when we looked back, the food truck was already gone.

TERIYAKI-DO: THE WAY OF TERIYAKI
Review: Larry's Lounge

Larry's Lounge is easy to find, just a block north of the Tom Douglas district in Belltown. You can go to Larry's for the ambiance (outlandishly velvet seats, gold-rimmed mirrored walls); you can go there for the liquor (five-time winner of a certain local alternative weekly's Blushing Lush award). You can even go there for the service (attentive to servile, border- ing on stalker), but Pat and I go for Larry's signature dish—the Chicken Larryaki.

A purist would be horrified; there is nothing teriyaki about the Larryaki. It's not even chicken. It's a whole Cornish game hen, glazed with Larry's special sweet soy-sake mixture and roasted with a bottle of sauce tucked into the cavity, basted with more sake, and then *lit on fire at the table*. It is total, unabashed Gimmick McGimmicksford, Scion of Gimmicks- ville, worse than Love & ChocoLatté's ill-conceived Bacon Sriracha Dark Chocolate Mocha or the disastrous StarKist™ and Ritz™ crackers spicy roll at Mooshi Sooshi. But, unlike the others, Larry's Chicken Larryaki is executed so perfectly that the gimmick burns away with the sake, burns, burns until you're left with nothing but crispy sweet skin and tender moist meat. This dish shouldn't work, but it does. It's like a portrait so ugly, it's beautiful. It's like a movie so bad, it's good.

It's also hella tasty. If you want something less fowl, try the crab ravioli; the marsala cream sauce is impeccable, deli- cately framing the large pieces of well-stuffed, handmade pasta. The Vodka Asparagus in Twice-Fried Bacon makes a great appetizer.

No matter what you get, make sure to cap off with dessert and coffee. Pat and I usually split a slice of Chocolate Chambord Death and the Mini Cheesecake in Kirsch, and it's a sobering idea to miss Larry's extremely potent Amaretto coffee. It's boozier than your Aunt Kristen's rum balls at Christmas. Trust me.

2

MOM AND DAD were watching a Korean drama in the living room. They rose to greet us as we entered through the door from the garage.

"Sam, welcome home."

"Hi, Mom. Hi, Dad. Thanks." Sam gave both of them awkward hugs.

"I thought you were going to Patrick's house," Mom said. "I'm glad you're staying with your family instead. You're always welcome to be here."

"Thanks, Mom, but I'll probably go to Patrick's place tomorrow."

"Why, Samantha? Your parents love you very much. It will be more convenient for you to stay with us after your bridal shower."

"Mom, I don't want to talk about it. I'm only staying here tonight because Patrick's busy, okay? I'm going to go unpack."

"I put your dinner on the table."

"Thanks. I'll eat it later." Sam was already halfway up the stairs.

Mom muttered something bitter. Dad replied calmly and led her back to the couch. There was a plate of sliced fruit on the glass coffee table, apples and oranges and peaches skewered with toothpicks.

I curled up into the shabby comfort of our black leather recliner, then grabbed my MacBook off the end table. Google was useless; the phrase "THE BEST TERIYAKI IN SEATTLE" was proclaimed by many restaurants both in and out of the city and, to my intense disappointment, I got no hits on "goth food truck." I dropped a query on Chowhound, speared a piece of apple, and looked up at the Taiwanese-brand widescreen TV.

"What's going on?" I couldn't understand Korean and I couldn't read the Chinese subtitles, but I liked to watch the rakishly good-looking actors and actresses. Korean dramas were the current fad; one of my aunts had discovered the genre through a friend, and now the entire extended family was hooked. The current "it" series was more supernatural than usual, but it was still quite entertaining.

"That woman is having Jung-Hoon's baby," Dad explained. "But she's married to his brother, Jung-Hee."

"Ah."

"The brothers have been fighting since they were young kids. Jung-Hee challenged Jung-Hoon to a duel. Eun-Mi is trying to stop it because she loves both of them. But she doesn't know that Jung-Hoon was possessed by an evil spirit who fell in love with her also."

"Huh."

I heard Sam creep downstairs behind us, sneaking into the kitchen to get her dinner. A moment later, she crept back upstairs. Sigh. Mom and Sam were more alike than they were different—average height, athletic build, shoulder-length hair, martyr complex—but they didn't understand each other at all, and I hated being in the middle of it.

"Daisy, you should do your homework."

"Okay, Mom." I traded my MacBook for my Statistics textbook and notepad, clicked lead out of a mechanical pencil.

It was Friday night. The homework was so boring. I flipped to another page and started to sketch. Jung-Hee and Jung-Hoon were still waving their arms and guns at each other.

"Do you think Samantha wants any fruit?" Mom asked, as I worked on the page.

"I don't know."

"I'll bring it upstairs."

I snagged another apple slice before Mom picked up the plate and left the living room. In parallel, Jung-Hoon picked up a gun and left the scene.

Sketch, sketch, sketch.

"Daisy," my dad said.

I looked up. "What?"

"What are you drawing?"

"Nothing." I looked down at the page, saw that I'd drawn a wooden ship with large, billowing sails in rocky waters. Two stick figures stood in the crow's nest and a stick deckhand stood on the deck with a stick parrot on his shoulder. There was a short flag at the top of the mast bearing the image of a bowl of chicken teriyaki and a pair of chopsticks.

Dad leaned over. "It looks pretty good." He pointed at the flag. "What's this?"

"Just thinking about food, I guess."

"It reminds me of a place where I ate dinner once." He turned back to the television. Eun-Mi and Jung-Hee were having a heated conversation about something, probably the baby, because Jung-Hee kept motioning at Eun's belly.

"What place?" I added a school of stick-fish below the waves, quick lazy scribbles moving in a diamond pattern, then started to draw a round whale floating above them.

"It was in Kent, when I first moved to Seattle. I was driving back from a client's office and I saw a strange food truck with a pirate ship on the side. The client was trying to cheat me and I was very, very mad."

"What?" I sat up straight, pencil down, whale unfinished.

"Hold on one moment, please. Eun-Mi is about to tell Jung-Hee about the baby's true father."

"Dad!" I'd lost him until the commercial break. Fuming, I sunk deeper into my seat and finished the whale, topping it off with a spigot of water splashing from its hump. I crossed out its eyes, added jagged teeth—*zombie* whale.

On-screen, Jung-Hee's face transformed from disbelief to anger. He seemed to push his bangs back a lot. Eun-Mi was on her knees, sobbing dramatically, her hands clasped tightly as she begged forgiveness. I rolled my eyes as Eun-Mi's voice rose higher and higher, imploring, "Jung-Hee, Jung-Hee." He cut her off.

The camera panned to the shadows, revealing a sinister-looking figure watching the unhappy couple—Jung-Hoon, the younger brother. His eyes glowed red as a dramatic orchestral sting swelled in the background. Cut to commercial.

"Okay, Dad, what happened in Kent?"

"Kent?"

"You said you found a strange food truck after getting cheated by a client in Kent a long time ago."

"Oh yes. The client was a very bad man. He never paid me. I had to write it off. It was a major headache. He took advantage of me. Now, I tell all of my clients to pay me in advance."

"No, Dad, what about the food truck?" Parents could be so frustrating sometimes.

"The food truck? Somebody painted a picture of a ship on it. The ship was filled with rice, like a bowl. It was just a picture, but it was very funny. There was a man working at the truck with long black hair and black clothes, and he charged me three dollars. Remember, Daisy, back then everything didn't cost so much."

"How did it taste?"

"Very good. It was the best meal I ever had."

"Really!"

"Yes." He hesitated. "But Daisy, they gave me a punch card, so I could not go back."

"Oh." Dad had few idiosyncrasies, but the strangest was his moral opposition to loyalty punch cards. He was convinced that they meant the restaurant was marking up the price. I still remember the day his favorite restaurant broke his heart by telling him, with much excitement, that they'd started rewarding customers with a free appetizer after every five meals. Sam and I used to order takeout from there on his birthday and pretend it came from a different store. Their eggplant in garlic sauce was pretty good.

I twirled my pencil, thinking. "Did the guy have a really low, hollow voice?"

"Hollow? What do you mean?"

"Um, kind of dry?" I adjusted my voice, rasping. "Hoarse? Like this."

"Mmm." Dad closed his eyes. "It was many years ago. That time, I didn't even meet your mom yet, Daisy."

"Was he very tall?" I continued to rasp.

"He was pretty tall," Dad conceded.

"And there was a bell, when they served? Not a normal bell, like, ding, but a loud, long chime, like bonnng?" I mimicked the sound.

"Yes, like that, bonnng."

"I think I saw him!"

"Oh? You did? In Kent?"

"No, in Issaquah. Sam and I went to get ice cream, and we saw a gray truck serving teriyaki on the other side of the parking lot."

"How did it taste?"

"Pretty good, but I need to try it again. Not as good as Ducky Teriyaki."

He nodded. "I thought I imagined it."

"I thought so, too. It disappeared really quickly. Sam and I didn't even hear it drive away after we got our food."

"Hmm." Dad turned back to the television. I sighed and put my notebook back down, opened my MacBook back up.

A few minutes later, Mom came pounding down the stairs. "Samantha is *your* daughter!" she shouted, throwing the fruit plate onto the table. I rescued an orange segment, trying to ignore her outburst. My computer chimed, and an IM window opened with Sam. I started to feel a little queasy. Maybe it was just the teriyaki.

LawGirl83: OMG
Me: What?
LawGirl83: I CAN'T BELIEVE MOM JUST DID THAT.
Me: What happened?

"Mei-Fung, what happened?" Dad asked. "You should be happy that Sam is staying with us tonight."

LawGirl83: I'M SO MAD AT HER.

"She cannot marry that boy. He is no good for her. I try to give her other options, but Sam will not listen to me." Mom looked *exactly* like Sam at the airport.

"Wait, what do you mean, other options?" I asked, feeling even queasier. It wasn't the teriyaki.

"My college friend has a son, very smart. He went to Stanford. My friend told me he is a very successful doctor in Manhattan. Sam could meet him for dinner. He is Sam's age. He doesn't have a girlfriend yet. His name is also Sam."

LawGirl83: SHE'S TRYING TO SET ME UP WITH ANOTHER GUY.

I was horrified. "Mom, you can't ask Sam to go on a date with someone. She's getting married in three months. Right, Dad?" He was staring at the carpet, avoiding eye contact with either of us.

"I just want her to give my friend's son a chance," Mom insisted. Her lips were tight. "I don't want Sam to make a mistake with Patrick."

LawGirl83: PATRICK AND I HAVE BEEN DATING FOR SIX YEARS.
LawGirl83: WE'RE GETTING MARRIED IN THREE MONTHS!!!
Me: Hold on.

"There's no chance to give, Mom. She's already engaged. Besides, they've been dating for six years. Sam knows what she's doing."

"Patrick is no good," she insisted. There was no use arguing with her.

"Mei-Fung, you can't interfere with Sam's wedding," Dad said, trying anyway. "Sam has to make her own choices. She's twenty-eight years old. She is her own woman."

"I wish she didn't go to Brown. She should have gone to UW. This is your fault for letting her go to the East Coast. She is too independent."

"Mei-Fung, we couldn't stop her. It was the right choice for her."

"I wish I didn't have her!" Mom shouted. She wasn't a Tiger Mom—more like a squirrel—but she could be just as dramatic.

"Mei-Fung, don't say that. You don't mean it."

Me: She's giving her "I wish you'd gone to UW / you're not my daughter" rant again.
LawGirl83: @$*&^*@&^
LawGirl83: Can you drive me to Patrick's place?
Me: I guess. Are you sure?
LawGirl83: Yes.
LawGirl83: No. DAMMIT. $#*&^*@!&$^
LawGirl83: Ugh. I'm still mad at Patrick, too. Dammit.
Me: *hug*

"I'm going to bed," I announced. "Good night."

I stopped by the kitchen on my way up to grab some cookies from one of my favorite local bakeries.

Knock, knock.

"What?" Sam called, sullen.

"It's me."

Like Mom, Sam didn't cry pretty; her eyes were red and her cheeks were wet and puffy. I offered her a cookie and a cold glass of milk.

"Thanks."

Erica's Bakery made the best cookies—crispy on the outside and chewy on the inside, each golden-brown cookie the size of your hand, each soft bite dripping richly with butter and salty-sweet caramel. I'd zapped them for fifteen seconds in the microwave, and the dark chocolate chunks were still melt-in-your-mouth warm. We ate them over napkins so we wouldn't lose the crumbs.

"Maybe I should go to dinner with Mom's friend."

"Seriously?" My sister, really. Sometimes, I wondered if she ever listened to herself.

"I don't know." Sam sighed dramatically. I rolled my eyes (they were getting quite a workout this evening).

"Sam, you're getting married in three months. You and Patrick are perfect for each other. Stop worrying about it."

"What if Mom's right? I'm giving up a great job for him. I'm a fourth-year associate at, like, the top-ranked corporate law firm in the U.S. We can't even figure out where to live together."

"I'm sure you guys will work it out. Pat's a great person. He's just a little bit of a jerk sometimes. Like everyone."

"Maybe." She looked skeptical and sad.

"If you want, you can borrow my car tomorrow. I'll just need you to drop me off at work."

"Sure."

"Cheer up. Everything's going to be fine. You're just a little mad right now."

"Yeah. All right. Thanks, Daisy."

"Good night, Sam." I collected our trash and shut the door behind me.

3

I WORKED ON THE weekends so it wouldn't interfere with school. Sam dropped me off a few hours before the lunch rush and promised to fetch me after another one of my teriyaki-filled shifts in suburbia.

There's an art to teriyaki. I know you're rolling your eyes, but it's true. Mediocre teriyaki joints are a dime a dozen, but good teriyaki restaurants are diamonds in the rough. You need to use good cuts of meat (preferably chicken thighs); you need to tenderize with a mallet; you need to marinate for at least an hour to get the most flavor into the finished product. Many places use a pre-made commercial sauce they buy in bulk, but we make our own sauce in-house every morning, a special blend of soy, mirin, honey, and garlic, plus a mysterious secret ingredient which I refuse to reveal even under threat of torture. I couldn't betray my boss; she's been too good to me.

I don't even remember how I found the job. It was probably on Craigslist, somewhere between an egg donor ad and a solicitation for reality television show contestants who have trouble getting rid of clutter. I'd never even heard of the place, but the location wasn't too far from home, the pay wasn't too bad, and the hours weren't too horrible. Plus, they said they'd train me. So, one day, five years ago, I met Nancy Uematsu at Uematsu House in downtown Renton, and she asked me why I wanted the job.

"To be honest, I'm looking for anything," I said. "I like teriyaki, I guess, so I thought I'd apply."

"You have no college degree?" she asked, checking my application again.

"No, sorry. I graduated from high school last year."

"I see."

She looked up again, gave me an intense once-over, and asked me about my cooking experience.

"I'm really good at following instructions," I said. "I can cook almost anything from a package."

Uematsu-san clucked disapproval. "What else can you do?"

"Um, do you have an apple? Or any vegetables?"

She found me a carrot, thick and orange, slightly gnarled and covered in dry skin. I borrowed a knife and began to carve, pretty basic stuff, just some frilly coin designs I'd learned from YouTube, but she was still impressed.

"It's easier with a carrot curler," I apologized.

Uematsu-san didn't hire me as a cook, but she did hire me to staff the register and wait the tables, and to make a backlog of carrot garnishes when the restaurant was slow. She was pretty mean with a paring knife herself, and she taught me a few garnishes I'd never even seen online.

The kitchen was clearly the most interesting place in the restaurant. I spent months admiring the kitchen crew, sneaking peeks behind the counter to watch the flames rise from their hot stoves, eavesdropping on their conversations and envying their laughter. The front of the restaurant was lonely, and when it was slow and I ran out of carrots, I didn't have much to do except draw. I practiced a lot of charcoal back then.

One year after I started, Uematsu-san found me in the dining room and said, "Come with me."

I'd already learned garnishes. I was upgraded to onions. One of the older line cooks, Jay, teased me about it, telling me that they'd asked Uematsu-san to bring me into the kitchen so they wouldn't have to cry so much. Jay's still with Uematsu House; he's Uematsu-san's right-hand man and one of my favorite people, a big Colombian guy with an even bigger smile and a teenage daughter, the joy of his life.

As far as prep work went, onions were a bit of a downgrade, truthfully. Garnishes are an art; they require aesthetics and dexterity and their value is in their beauty. Onions are food; you can chop an onion any which way and no one will really care as long as you have chunks (or slices, or minced bits, whatever you're told). They're getting covered in sauce anyway.

At some point, Uematsu-san made me get a food handler's permit and, suddenly, I was doing *everything*.

It was awesome. I'd never cooked much before, and now I was cooking all the time. I loved the heat of the stove, standing next to its hot glow and navigating a large pan around it. I loved the sounds and sizzles; I loved the smell of fresh vegetables and slightly charred meat. I loved the magic of cooking, the alchemy of combining fire and raw ingredients to create tasty, edible food. I even loved the onions, tears and all. There was something empowering about chopping my way through a full box of large yellow sweets, seeing myself fill our tubs with mounds of onion pieces. It was hot, tiring work, but I loved working with my hands, cooking chicken and crafting meals.

On Saturdays, I usually shared the kitchen with Jay. Alice, one of Uematsu-san's Japanese exchange students, usually worked the counter. She wasn't required for prep though, so Alice usually showed up right at opening.

"*Ohayo!*" I greeted as I walked in the front door.

"*Ohayo!*" Jay called back. I could hear him chopping vegetables in the kitchen, efficient, clockwork, thock-thock-thock.

Uematsu House was fairly small; most of our customers came for take-out. We sat fifty in the main area, four tables of four along each side and three tables of six down the middle, with a few chairs and a pile of old newspapers near the register for the take-out customers. The kitchen was directly behind the counter, a tight area with limited space for cutting, but there were four large burners and a big steel freezer. Around the corner, there was a single large unisex restroom and a small storage closet with cleaning supplies.

I tossed my backpack into the locked cabinet under the register, then grabbed an apron and washed my hands.

"I already made the sauce," Jay said, and I nodded, pulling on a pair of gloves. I went to the fridge to get the chicken.

At Uematsu House, we didn't offer very many dishes. It was a straightforward matrix—meat × carb × sauce. The options were pretty limited: we offered beef, chicken, and tofu; white/brown rice and yakisoba; teriyaki and spicy teriyaki. Uematsu-san had tried offering ramen once, but people weren't interested. We'd dumped gallons of stock every night, and no one noticed when we took it off the menu. We also served pan-fried gyoza (stuffed in-house) and salted boiled edamame as part of the daily combination special, and we offered chicken-katsu on Sundays.

Prep wasn't too bad. We served the teriyaki with onions and a side of salad, the yakisoba with steamed vegetables. Uematsu-san sourced most of her ingredients from a local farmer, and the food wasn't complicated. It was just simple, tasty, filling. The secret, as they say, was in the sauce.

"How are you doing, Jay?" Raw chicken was slimy, but I was used to it, and it helped to wear the gloves. I tore the plastic wrap off the first styrofoam container and pulled out a thigh.

"Feeling pretty good. How about yourself?"

"I'm all right. Sam's in town this weekend. We're having her bridal shower tomorrow."

"Nice."

We prepped in amiable silence. Chicken was pretty straightforward as long as you weren't afraid of it. At Uematsu House, we cooked ours skin-on, but we did have to debone the pieces to make fillets.

Finished with another package of chicken, I dumped the meat into a large plastic bin and chased it with thick, sweet sauce. I stuck on the lid and put it back in the fridge.

"Oh, Jay, I gotta tell you about this food truck."

"Yeah?" Jay shared my hobby and I think he's the only person I know who's eaten more teriyaki than I have. He looked up from a cutting board full of beef.

"Oh yeah. You'll love it. Sam and I found this totally weird teriyaki food truck in Issaquah, can you believe that? The guy who ran it was really tall, long hair, short beard, kinda like a goth pirate. He said he was cursed."

"C'mon, you're pulling my leg." Jay smiled and shook his head.

"No way, I'm totally serious."

"Well, then, how was the food?"

"I thought it was pretty good. Sam said it was too sweet."

Jay snorted. "Sam thinks everything tastes too sweet. Sam thought our steamed vegetables were too sweet." In Sam's defense, I had accidentally spilled honey all over the broccoli on the exact day she decided to go see where Daisy works. Oops.

"I dunno, sometimes Sam has a pretty good taste-sense," I said. "She was always the first one in the house to figure out when the milk went bad."

"Mmm."

The door chimed. It was 10:45 a.m., and it was Alice.

"*Ohayo!*" she greeted in her perky, happy voice.

"*Ohayo!*" we called back.

Alice Nakano was a pretty girl, which helped business, but not as much as Uematsu-san's special sauce. Like many of Uematsu-san's past disciples, Alice was living with Uematsu-san through a cultural exchange program that allowed her to study in the United States. Alice had adopted an American name and was practicing English by reading books she'd checked out from the library. She loved American culture, especially baseball, and she thought Ichiro was *dreamy*; Alice never missed a Seattle Mariners game.

"*Genki desu ka?*" I practiced.

"Awesome *desu*," she replied enthusiastically. "Lulu is in town with the baby. Uematsu-san is taking them to the zoo today."

Lulu was Uematsu-san's only daughter, Sam's age and married with a three-year-old son who was spoiled rotten by his grandmother. They had recently moved to Spokane, on the other side of the state, and Uematsu-san tried to see them as often as she could.

"Oh, that's good. It's too bad Lulu moved away. I liked her a lot."

"Me too," Jay said.

It was pretty quiet for a Saturday, but that was okay. Jay and I joked in the kitchen, trading stories about our families, while Alice read in the front. Jay's own daughter was starting high school in the fall, and he was mock-nervous about it, lamenting that he'd need to keep an eye on the boys. I assured him that she would be fine.

"Daisy, why don't you do your homework?" Jay suggested between lunch and dinner.

I made a face, but I obediently took the notebook out of my backpack and opened it up.

Yesterday's pirate ship doodle was still on the page. I smoothed out the paper and held it out; not too bad. Kind of cute, I guess. I'd bothered to draw the wooden grain-lines on the ship, and the sails were pro even for me, billowing quite convincingly. I drew a large cloud in the sky, wide-cheeked with two closed eyes, blowing into the sail.

Strangely, there was no one in the crow's nest, and three people on the deck. I thought I'd drawn them in different positions last night... I must have misremembered.

I slogged through a statistics problem, then switched to sketching Alice instead. She looked up and grinned, then turned back to her book.

By mutual agreement, we closed early. Wiping down tables, I looked outside briefly, watching the orange glow of the setting sun fall across the suburban strip malls around us. I blinked and looked again. For a moment, I thought I saw a dark food truck across the street, next to the gas station. But it must have been my imagination, because there was nothing there.

TERIYAKI-DO: THE WAY OF TERIYAKI
Review: Teriyaki.NET

Pat says that only a group of ex-Microsoft programmers could have started a place like Teriyaki.NET.

Me: "I don't get it."

Pat: "It's a coding thing. You see, dot-NET is a Microsoft software framework. Sometimes, when people create projects, they'll call them 'whatever-dot-NET.' Ex-Apple employees would've called it iTeriyaki."

Me: "Patrick, you're such a dork."

Sometimes Patrick and I like to play a game called "If I Owned This Restaurant."

"If I owned this restaurant," starts Patrick, "I wouldn't call my teriyaki special 'Cyber Chicken.' It's too 1998. It doesn't fit the dot-NET theme at all."

"If I owned this restaurant," I say, "I wouldn't call it Color.Brown rice. That's just dumb."

"If I owned this restaurant," continues Patrick, "I wouldn't charge ten dollars for substandard beef yakisoba. If I really need to charge ten dollars to make a modest profit, I must be using the wrong suppliers. I'd get a different beef supplier anyway. This meat is too tough."

"If I owned this restaurant," I suggest, "I wouldn't buy my teriyaki sauce from Costco. Nothing against Costco, I just think a chef should come up with her own sauce. Seriously, people, it's not rocket science."

"If I owned this restaurant," offers Patrick, "I wouldn't treat my staff members so poorly. This place has the surliest clerks in Puget Sound. It's not natural. The owner must be abusing them."

"If I owned this restaurant," I comment, "I wouldn't cook the chicken so dry. This stuff is gross. I can feel it sucking all the moisture out of my mouth. Ugh."

"If I owned this restaurant," concedes Patrick, "I would keep the location. It's in a pretty good spot. The menu needs more documentation, though. At least the first item is 0."

It's true—Teriyaki.NET is in prime Microsoft territory, and despite the existence of no fewer than seven higher-quality teriyaki places within a three-block radius, it seems to attract more than its fair share of customers. I don't know why. Maybe they're coming here in solidarity, showing support for their former coworkers who managed to escape the corporate grind. Maybe they're coming for the salad dressing, which is the only thing of any redeeming value on the menu—very gingery and only a little bit sweet, thin enough to flow and thick enough to stick. Maybe they're coming here just so they can stop by the Cookietopia next door when they're done. Or maybe they're just too lazy to walk across the street.

Last I heard, the owners were planning to open another restaurant called "Thai Catch Finally." Pat thinks this is hilarious. I still don't get it, and really, I'm okay with that.

4

PATRICK WAS BACK in town. He and Sam must have seen each other and already made up, because she was glowing when she came back early with my car.

"Can you drop me off at Patrick's condo?" she asked. "I already put my stuff in the trunk."

"Sure."

I didn't tell Sam about seeing the food truck again—I knew I must have imagined it. Still, I jumped online as soon as I got home. Chowhound was intrigued but unhelpful; several commenters said they'd keep an eye out, and one or two people suggested other, non-goth teriyaki trucks (all of which I'd already tried). Disappointed, I closed my laptop and went to bed.

Sam's bridal shower was pure elegance and good breeding—well, almost. The scones were fresh, the tea was hot, and the bride was downright cheerful. Sam's friends and our cousins brought lively conversation and gifts beautifully wrapped in silver and pink. Even Mom couldn't keep herself from smiling.

In fact, Mom was so excited that she couldn't help sharing other happy news.

"Juliet," she said, addressing one of our older cousins. "We are so excited to hear about the baby."

Our cousin paled. "What do you mean?" Juliet didn't look pregnant at all.

"Your baby. Your mom told me yesterday. We are so happy to hear that there will be another member of the family soon."

Aunt May reddened and said something sharply to Mom in Taiwanese.

Mom laughed. "Oh, I forgot it was a secret. I'm so sorry."

"Congratulations, Juliet," Sam said, and then swiftly changed the subject back to her law firm interview on Monday to spare our cousin further embarrassment.

Due to logistics involving Patrick/Sam schedule constraints, I found myself driving Sam back to the airport on Monday night.

"Did you know that Juliet was pregnant?" I asked.

"Nope. Mom has such a big mouth sometimes."

"Yeah. How did your interview go?"

"Bombed it." To my surprise, Sam didn't look concerned at all. I didn't believe her anyway; Sam was incapable of failing anything.

"What are you going to do?"

"I have a phone interview with Natalie's firm next week."

Natalie was one of Sam's old roommates, a gorgeous bombshell from Hong Kong with a hot British accent that caused men to drool. (We've tested this in bars.) She moved to Seattle after law school and was a rising associate at a medium-size firm specializing in technology startups.

"In Queen Anne?"

"Yeah. Well, her firm has a San Francisco office, too. Both, I guess."

"Does that mean you're moving to San Francisco?"

"Patrick and I are still discussing it." She sounded neutral.

"Right."

"We're both keeping an open mind about it."

"Sure." Sam was smart. She knew what she was doing, especially when it came to Patrick.

Despite the unresolved geographical question, the wedding wasn't in jeopardy—yet. Planning, at least, was still going on, because Sam called me a few days later to run an errand.

"What?"

"Can you and Mom talk to the wedding planner this week and double-check on the deposit for the florist? Patrick and I already picked out the flowers. I totally forgot."

"Can't Mom go by herself?"

"She's going to change the flower arrangements."

"Sam, you're so ridiculous. Mom wouldn't do that."

"Well, I need you to tell Mom to check on the deposit. Patrick's parents are taking care of the catering, and Mom and Dad promised they'd pay for everything else."

"Why don't you tell her yourself? Or ask Dad? Or use a credit card?"

"Daisy, I just need this one thing, okay?"

"Fine."

"I'll email the information to you."

I resolved to forward it to Mom and wash my hands of the entire situation.

Predictably, Mom wanted to know why Sam couldn't talk to her herself if she expected her to pay for the wedding.

"It's no good," she said, disapproving. "Samantha is too independent."

I sighed, got the check from Dad, and drove to the wedding planner's office myself, all in the name of family harmony. On the phone, Sam's wedding planner had sounded absolutely vicious, and I couldn't wait to meet her in person.

Hilde Sørensdóttir was even more imposing than I'd imagined. She was big, tall, and clad in a dark-red power suit. She wore her hair in long yellow pigtails, and she possessed an ample bosom. In a fight, she would totally kick my ass.

She glared down at me, towering above my small self, demanding to know who I was. I resisted the urge to cower. From my vantage point far below her, I had a great view of the simple, yet beautiful, red-gold ring she wore on her right hand.

"Daisy Wang," I replied. I felt my legs quiver slightly. "We spoke yesterday. I have a deposit for my sister, Samantha." Clearly, this woman ruled her vendors through fear, not love.

"Very well. Come with me."

Hilde led me through a short hallway with bare white walls and motioned me into a posh leather chair in a small office.

"Here." I found Dad's check and put it on the table.

"Thank you," she said, softening slightly. "Let me make you a copy and get you the receipt." For such a large woman, she moved quite nimbly.

I sighed audibly when she left the room. Relaxing, I leaned back in my chair and took a look around.

The office was well-decorated and lit brightly by the sun from the unshaded windows. Hilde used a large oak executive's desk, which she kept quite tidy. Behind her extremely large leather executive's chair there hung a trio of small oil paintings, separated a few inches apart, depicting a beautiful black raven in flight, its wings spread across the tableau. For a wedding planner's office, I would have put up a white dove instead, but I guess that wasn't Hilde's style.

The raven was oddly compelling. I felt mesmerized by its gaze, its head cocked toward the viewer, its eyes glowing dark and red. The backdrop behind it was thickly textured, a mystical coral pink sky with swirling clouds and no sun. It really was a beautiful piece.

I swiveled my chair around and gasped. On the wall behind me, there was a huge abstract painting in magentas and carmines, which made me want to cry in a way I couldn't explain, something about the impression of tears streaming from a small shape in the center of the work, or maybe it was the colors... It wasn't appropriate for a wedding planner's office either; the figure was too lonely. This office should have been decorated in cupids and hearts and kittens, or some kind of gothic Victorian theme, not full-fledged, abstract despair. I looked away to break the gut-punching feeling and turned to Hilde's tall antique oak bookshelves instead, reading the names off the spines.

I expected things like *Best Romantic Spots* 2011 and bridal dress catalogs, but Hilde's tastes were either more sophisticated, or more for show. The books ran eclectic and slightly New Age. I saw philosophy books, cultural studies, mythology and folklore, anthropology textbooks, even several volumes on ancient contracts law. There was a shelf devoted to nothing but supernatural events, another focused on religious studies (beneath a shelf with books on spiritualism), and a long bottom shelf with tall, beautiful art books. It reminded me of a used bookstore that Sam and I had once seen in Providence, which offered to price books by the yard rather than content or rarity.

One of the art books caught my eye. I went to the shelf and crouched to inspect it, a dark scarlet tome. The spine was nameless but gilded in intricate gold, featuring delicate vines in an Art Nouveau style climbing up the text. I reached forward to touch it, then stopped myself.

Hilde was coming back down the hall.

I moved back to my seat and put my hands politely in my lap.

The door opened. Hilde appeared with a red manila folder. "Here's a copy of the check, and here's the receipt. Please give these to your sister."

"Thanks. You'll get the check to the vendor?"

"Yes, I'll take care of it."

"Um, thanks." I smiled. "I guess I'll be going now."

"Let me lead you out."

"Although, can I ask—"

"Yes?" Full gaze, impatient, a ghost of a tapping foot.

Bravely: "Who painted that gorgeous triptych behind you?" I cocked my head at the raven. "It's so beautiful. The expression is hypnotic."

Hilde relaxed, rewarded me with a smile. "I did."

"Oh cool. What about that abstract piece?" I turned around and motioned to it. It hurt to look at so I quickly turned back. "I didn't realize you could do that with abstract art. I mean, unless you're Picasso. There's so much raw emotion."

"Also mine."

My jaw dropped. "You're awesome. Have you ever exhibited?"

"Quite frequently, in my youth. But I have not painted in many decades."

"That's a shame. I wish I had a tenth of your skill."

"Many people do," she said, leading me out.

I suppose arrogance is inevitable where one finds talent. Still, Hilde's art was inspiring, and I resolved to paint as soon as I got home. I mused on subjects, wondering if I should try my own abstract piece. I walked back to my car, threw Sam's photocopies on the passenger seat, looked up, and stopped.

The goth teriyaki truck was parked across the street.

I jumped out of the car and slammed the door, then swore. This was a busy intersection. I waited impatiently as a large semi came rushing down the street, rattling me with its loud engine. It was followed by a King County Metro bus, a large yellow Hummer, a Seattle public school bus, another semi, a tanker truck, and, finally, a third semi.

By the time the street had cleared, the food truck was already gone.

5

THIS FOOD TRUCK thing was really starting to bug me. I'd been dreaming about it all week, and now I'd seen or hallucinated it twice more without getting a chance to eat there again. There was something about it, about the transient nature of the food, about the weird (but strangely attractive) staff, about the cheesy pirate-teriyaki-bowl picture, that made me desperate to find it. Besides, I liked to try a place two or three times before I pronounced official judgment on my blog.

Sam killed her phone interview with Natalie's law firm, and they flew her out for an in-person interview a few weeks later. I caught her on the phone at Patrick's place.

"What's up?" When Sam was happy, she was more benevolent than the queen of England.

"Nothing."

She waited.

"It's that stupid food truck. I keep seeing it everywhere. It's totally creeping me out."

"Go on."

"I dreamt about it last night, too, I think. I don't know. I just remember food and danger." And a tall, dark-haired man with a short beard and sad, desperate eyes.

"Daisy, you always dream about food."

"Geez, I don't *always* dream about food."

"Fine, you don't *always* dream about food. If it's bugging you so much, why don't we go back?"

Fair enough. The next day, Patrick dropped her off at our house after work.

"Remind me, where are you guys going again?" he asked.

I looked over at Sam. She was typing quickly on her Blackberry, ignoring us.

"Issaquah," I replied. "We're hunting down a teriyaki truck. Wanna come?"

He shook his head. "I'd love to, but I have to get back to the office. My boss gets lonely if there's no one around to flog."

"Are you sure? It's 'THE BEST TERIYAKI IN SEATTLE.' At least, that's what the sign said."

"Yeah, right. Where have I heard that before? Kawaii Bento?" We both shuddered.

"Seriously, though, it's pretty good. Right, Sam?"

She looked up. "It was too sweet."

"That's because you're so sweet, you contaminate everything you touch, you snugglemuffin," Patrick said.

"Yes dear," she said dismissively, then kissed him anyway.

I stuck my tongue out. "We need to go before you guys make me throw up."

Sam rolled her eyes at me, then turned back to her fiancé. "Bye, dear," she said. "Don't work too hard."

"You too. Put your email away, hon."

She kissed him again and put the Blackberry back into her purse, taking it back out as soon as she got in my car.

"How's the job search going?" I asked.

"Hold on, I'm almost done."

"Okay." I switched from talking to singing along to the radio.

Three songs later, Sam tucked her smartphone away. "Well, Patrick is pretty sure that Diego will hire him."

"Cool."

"If I'm careful about it, I think I can get Natalie's firm to hire me into their California office instead of Seattle. I have an interview tomorrow."

"That's good. I'm sure you'll do a great job."

We reached the strip mall. To our disappointment, the parking lot was empty.

"Maybe the people at the ice cream store can help," Sam suggested. She probably just wanted more ice cream. Sam ordered a kid's scoop of honey lavender; I ordered nothing.

"Daisy, what's wrong with you? Do you want to try some?"

"No. I guess I'm not hungry."

"Hmm." She stared at me hard, then turned to our cute female teenage server. "How often does that teriyaki food truck show up in this plaza? Is there a schedule?"

"Food truck?" The teenager looked confused.

"Yes, food truck. A truck that serves food. Like an ice cream truck, but with hot food? Taco truck? Mobile kitchen? Roach coach?"

"Sorry, I don't know what you're talking about." She smiled.

"Look—" Sam checked the girl's name badge. "Madison. It's a huge gray truck with a picture of a pirate teriyaki ship on the side. How could you miss it? We saw it a few weeks ago. How long have you worked here? Is there anyone else in the store?"

Madison shook her head vigorously, still smiling. It was Monday evening, and she was the only one on shift. Sam sighed dramatically, then led us out of the store.

"What is wrong with these people?" She scooped a vicious spoonful of ice cream. "Are you sure you don't want any? It's pretty good."

"I'm fine." The girl's response had been strange. I didn't think she was hiding anything, but she'd acted pretty suspiciously.

Sam must have come to the same conclusion, because as soon as she finished her ice cream she said, "That kid was useless. Let's ask around."

We started with the next store on the block, the nail salon. It was too bright inside, garishly lit. I squinted, following Sam as she led us into what had to be the most low-budget salon in the whole of Puget Sound. There were soft, gentle recliners—if you considered bright blue dentist's chairs to be soft and gentle. (At least they reclined.) There was a series of ugly overhead lamps along a bank of tables set aside for decorative nail work. There was a pathetic bubbling fountain near the cash register making soft noises. On further inspection, it bore a strong resemblance to one of the basins at my dentist's office. The entire store looked like someone had gone crazy at a dentist office surplus sale.

"Can I help you?"

Sam is tall for our family, but I'm pretty short. Even still, I had to look down at the petite, middle-aged woman who had greeted us.

Sam jumped in immediately. "Hi. We're looking for some information about this shopping plaza."

The woman smiled at us. "We have a special today, just for you two lovely girls. Mani-pedi at a discount price. Only thirty dollars."

"Thank you, we really appreciate the offer, but we're not here to do our nails. We just have a question."

"You don't want mani-pedi?" The woman tsked loudly. Before I could stop her, she grabbed my right hand. "Look. She has such beautiful hands, but her nails are so rough. Look at how rough." She shoved my hand at Sam, tapping at the nails.

"Hey!" I jerked my hand back. I didn't care if my hands were smooth and youthful, or if they looked like wrinkled, vulturous claws. If I could draw, chop, and cook, they were good enough for me.

"Please, we just have a question," Sam said. "Have you seen a food truck parked around here? It serves chicken teriyaki. My sister really liked the food and we're trying to find it again."

"I don't have time for idle chitchat."

"We just want to know if you've seen the truck."

"I have seen a food truck here," the woman said. "But I cannot tell you more unless you order a mani-pedi."

"That's ridiculous. Just tell us what you know. Please."

The woman shook her head. "You should order service or leave. I suggest mani-pedi. Otherwise your skin will be rough and no one will marry you."

Sam negotiated us down to pedicures only, express. She was masterful, but the salon woman was a tough opponent, pointing out that she could call another girl over to do our hands while someone worked on our feet. Sam held her ground and countered that she was already getting two customers, which meant her gossip had better be twice as good, and besides, we didn't have all night. Grudgingly, the salon woman showed us the polish selection and led us to the chairs.

They really were dentist's chairs. My gums ached just sitting in mine, and I could feel the hard cushion pressing against my back. Sam and Mom had been blessed with great teeth, but Dad and I attracted cavities like a new restaurant attracts food bloggers.

"Tell me more about the food truck," Sam said as the woman began to scrub her feet with pumice. "How often does it come here? We'd like to try the food."

The woman ignored her and started scrubbing harder. I watched with interest; my sister was a lawyer, but I'd never seen her interrogation skills at work. My own nail technician was much younger, probably my age, and she smiled too much.

"Ma'am, we had a deal. You said if my sister and I ordered salon services, you would tell us about the food truck. We just want to know the schedule."

The woman kept her head down. I watched all of Sam's goodwill disappear faster than daylight in a Seattle winter.

Then again, Sam did enjoy a challenge, and she was a former Washington All-State High School Junior Debate Club Champion.

"Look, just tell us something about it, please. Just tell us if it exists. Does it even exist?"

Scrub, scrub, scrub.

"You don't even have to say anything. Just nod. Once if you've seen the truck, twice if you haven't."

The woman switched to Sam's other foot. My own technician had already clipped my nails and moved on to painting. I had one foot in the lukewarm water, wondering about hygiene, as she tickled the other with a small brush full of polish.

"I don't know what game you're playing, but I really don't appreciate it. Please don't make me tell your manager."

How would Sam sound, trying to explain to the manager that she was upset because the older woman hadn't... What? Hadn't told us what she knew about a goth-looking pirate chicken teriyaki food truck that Sam and I may or may not have imagined in this random suburban strip mall?

My overachieving nail technician finished my left foot. She laid it on a scraggly terrycloth towel to dry and pulled my right foot out of the water. From my uncomfortable position on the chair, I wiggled my toes and admired the shimmering dark purple paint I'd chosen.

So quickly that I almost missed it, Sam's woman nodded once.

Sam gasped and tried to stand up. "You've seen it? When?"

The woman pushed her back into the chair. "Your feet are so ugly. I will make them beautiful."

"What—"

The woman returned to Sam's feet, head back down. Swiftly, she pulled one foot out of the water and began clipping.

"The truck comes rarely," she continued.

Sam leaned forward eagerly. "How rarely? Weekly?"

"Only at night. Once every few days. There is no schedule."

"Keep talking. When was the last time you saw it?"

"Yesterday. I ordered a chicken burrito."

"What?"

"The salsa was too mild," the woman said, putting Sam's foot back in the water. She pulled out the other foot. Click, click, click.

"Excuse me, are we talking about the same food truck? I specifically asked about chicken teriyaki, not burritos."

"The burritos are acceptable, but they need to add more spice."

My technician was working on a second coat. I felt her tug my pant leg and I looked down. "What?"

She smiled, then motioned toward the parking lot with a quick toss of her head. I stared through the large storefront windows.

"Sam," I hissed. Then, louder: "Sam!"

"What?"

"Outside. It's the truck."

It had gotten dark while we'd been trapped in the salon getting so-called "express" service. The truck seemed to be hiding in the shadows, an impression of a large unformed shape parked next to a lamppost. I felt myself fascinated and repulsed. Part of me wanted to run over and see it, but part of me was too paralyzed to move. My heart beat faster as a figure emerged from the back of the truck, moving to stand casually next to it.

"Your feet are so ugly," the older woman repeated, tsking again. She picked up the elegant red polish that Sam had chosen earlier and drew out a thick, wet brush.

"We're done," Sam said, trying to get up. The woman held her legs down, still trying to paint.

"Your nails are not done yet."

"I said we're done, okay?" Sam pushed herself to standing and pulled some cash out of her purse. "Here, this should cover both of us. I don't care if you don't finish."

The woman shook her head. "Your nails are not done yet," she repeated, still trying to paint.

"I don't care. Let me go."

I noticed a movement outside. It was Madison, our petite teenager, stepping outside the ice cream store and locking the door, and now clad in a long black coat with bright buttons and buckles. She looked around furtively, then began walking toward the truck.

Sam was still trying to get out of her chair. Sam ran marathons and worked weights at the gym, and she was getting bested by a woman twice her age, at least. Her manicurist was stronger and sprier than she looked. Somehow, the woman still managed to finish painting a foot, even as Sam struggled under her grip.

My technician pulled my pants leg again. "Done." She was still smiling.

"Thanks."

She patted my calves with the towel and motioned to a couch. I stood up and hesitated.

"Daisy," Sam shouted. "Get this woman off me."

I shook my head, falling out of the reverie. Then, shocked: "What the hell is going on?"

"This woman is crazy, that's what's going on."

I rushed over to them. The older woman was still muttering about the sorry state of Sam's skin as she continued to paint Sam's thrashing foot. From behind, I grabbed the woman around her waist and pulled her back.

For someone so small, she was heavy. Sam's toenails were covered in polish. So were Sam's toes, Sam's feet, the cuffs of Sam's jeans... Sam grunted and got herself out of the chair.

The truck was still outside. We all turned to watch as Madison from the ice cream shop handed a punch card and a wad of cash to Goth Teriyaki Truck Man. He stamped the punch card and returned her change, then handed her a large plastic bag. She flipped her hair, then walked away.

"I'm so sorry. Please forgive my employee."

I twisted to look behind me. A matronly woman had appeared next to a side door. She rushed over to us. I felt Sam's woman relax, and I let her go.

The matron spoke angrily to Sam's woman, then motioned to the door. Quickly, the other woman ran to the door and left, shutting it behind her.

"I am the owner," the matron said. "Please forgive my technician. Sometimes, she is too dedicated to her work."

"This is the worst nail salon I have ever visited," Sam said. Her eyes flashed, and she glared at the owner. "Give me one reason why I shouldn't sue you and your employee for assault right now."

"I'm so sorry." The new woman ran to the register. "Please, take these gift certificates. Good for two free full nail services, any time you want. Also, tonight is no charge."

"You better believe tonight is no charge," Sam shot back. She grabbed her purse from the dentist's chair. "Daisy, we're leaving now."

Our nails were still wet. We picked up our shoes and ran outside.

The truck was gone.

TERIYAKI-DO: THE WAY OF TERIYAKI
Review: Kei Teriyaki

Kei Teriyaki is a cute little shop near the Ballard Locks, made even cuter by its motto: "Where Everything Tastes O-Kei."

Pat: "I don't get it."

Me: "It's a bilingual pun. You see, in Japanese, 'o' is an honorific so it's like they're elevating the cook, but in English, it's just, like, okay."

Pat: "Daisy, you've been watching too much anime."

I don't know why everyone serves fish around the locks. I guess it's easy to get hungry for fish after you've watched so many of them passing through the fish ladder, chasing their deep primal fish instincts and the scent of their fishy home waters, swimming desperately for their fishy lives and the lives of their unborn fish children.

Kei Teriyaki is no exception. Pat and I usually trade off, one of us ordering chicken teriyaki and the other ordering salmon. If it's a sunny day, we'll get our food to go and find a quiet spot in the botanical gardens where we can make cynical hipster comments about all of the young families in the park. (SAM, I'M JOKING, PATRICK TOTALLY WANTS KIDS.)

I'm usually a chicken teriyaki sorta girl (duh), but my mouth waters just thinking of Kei's salmon teriyaki. If beef teriyaki is the jockish older brother of the teriyaki family, and chicken teriyaki is the bratty younger sister, then salmon teriyaki is the elegant matriarch, refined and tasteful, draped in an expensive silk dress and large shimmery pearls. (If you're unlucky, salmon teriyaki is tawdry and desperate, a deep-voiced chain smoker wearing too much makeup who's trying to relive some real or imagined youthful glory.)

Kei serves it like the matriarch. Here, the salmon is buttery and fresh, grilled with a sweet glaze of perfect consistency and quantity—like mixing in just enough blue to make the perfect green. The chicken is also pretty good, but sometimes, a girl just wants to be treated nice, y'know? They're both served with your choice of rice (white, brown, or fried, no extra charge) and cooked with a minimum of vegetables.

My only complaint is that Kei Teriyaki should offer a combination platter so I can get my chicken and salmon fix at the same time. Sometimes, I go by myself, and then I have to pick: Chicken or salmon? Chicken or salmon? I've tried getting both, but the leftovers just don't taste as good the next day. Then again, leftovers rarely do.

But really, you can't go wrong with either. Kei Teriyaki is more than O-Kei—it's good.

6

THE ICE CREAM shop denied any knowledge of anything when I called them the next morning.

"What food truck?" asked the man on the phone. "I don't know anyone here named Madison. Are you thinking of our store near Southcenter?"

Traffic was bad and I was late for class. Blah blah, class, ho hum, what is there to say? It was Tuesday, Statistics at noon and Philosophy at 1:30 p.m. I dragged my way through both, then headed back to Uematsu House to cover the afternoon shift.

Jay greeted me from the kitchen. The restaurant was dead in the middle of the afternoon, as usual. Alice was working the register again. I found her at a table, reading Tolkien.

"You like Tolkien?"

She laughed. "I read *Lord of the Rings* in Japanese when I was a teenager. I thought it would help." Cute pout. "It's not helping."

"How did they translate the Elvish?"

"With katakana, how do you say? Transliteration."

I put on an apron and fell into a carrot garnish-making role in lieu of anything else. Jay was organizing the ingredients shelf by frequency of use.

"Hey Daisy, did you ever find that truck again?"

"Oh, man. Sam and I went back to Issaquah, and there was this whole thing with this crazy lady at the nail salon. I don't want to talk about it." I grimaced.

"Sounds pretty exciting."

"You have no idea."

The dinner rush never came, and we closed early again. It was becoming a habit.

I was—dare I say—sick of teriyaki. Mom and Dad had already eaten when I got home, but Mom had left a covered plate for me on the kitchen table. It was Japanese-style curry—packaged curry cubes, water, and chopped chicken and vegetables thrown together in a crockpot for hours. Mom often cooked lazy when she was feeling stressed, and Sam's wedding was stressing everyone out.

The food was a little cold, so I threw it in the microwave and paced around the kitchen floor.

"Daisy, is Sam still in town?" Mom asked, entering the kitchen. "Maybe she can come to dinner with us tomorrow."

"I don't know. Why don't you call her and ask? I think her interview was today."

"I don't like to bother her. Is she at her boyfriend's house?"

"Her fiancé's house, and you know his name. It's okay, Mom, she doesn't mind."

"Can you call her?"

I grumbled, but I put my now-too-hot plate on the counter and took my iPhone out of my pocket.

"Yes?"

"Mom wants to know if you're coming to dinner tomorrow night." I tilted the speaker away from my mouth and blew on a spoonful of curry.

"Why doesn't she just call me?"

"I don't know. Are you coming or not?"

"No. I'm at the airport. My flight's boarding in half an hour. We can get dinner in a few weeks."

"All right." I passed the message on to Mom, who was obviously disappointed.

The curry was still too hot, but it was tasty and familiar. Growing up, it had been my favorite dish, and it was one of the first things I'd learned to prepare by myself. I wafted curry fumes into the living room and found Dad perched attentively in front of the TV.

"Eun-Mi is thinking about suicide," he explained. "She thinks it will fix the brothers' problem because then they will have nothing to fight over anymore."

"Great." Stupid patriarchy. I barfed quietly to myself. I didn't want Eun-Mi to sacrifice herself for the men's happiness, no matter how mopey and melodramatic she was. Besides, the brothers would probably kill each other as soon as she was dead.

"Hey, Dad. What do you think I should do with my life?"

He leaned back on the couch. "Daisy, it is up to you.

Obviously, your mom and I want you to be successful."

"I don't know what to do. The counselor told me I have to pick a major soon."

"Why don't you try accounting? It is a very good career. You can meet a lot of people."

I grimaced. "Dad, I'm not good at math. I don't want to do numbers for a living."

"Well, what do you want to do?"

"I told the counselor I wanted to draw. She suggested graphic design or architecture. I don't think I have the math for architecture."

He nodded. "Graphic design would be a good career. You can help me create brochures for my business."

"I guess." I didn't like the idea of three more years of school, and I didn't want a desk job, but I couldn't see any other options. Maybe I could study art history and become a curator.

On screen, the spirit-possessed Jung-Hoon, alerted to Eun-Mi's plans through a contrived and previously unexplained extra sense, stopped her as she stood on the brink of a cliff. I wished my own deus ex machina would arrive to save me from myself.

It was the first Thursday in October and Seattle museums were open and free. I hadn't been to the Wing Luke Museum in a while, and I was jonesing for a cheap and tasty dinner, so I drove down to the International District and found a good spot to park.

I didn't make it to dinner.

I was standing on the corner of Jackson and Maynard, wondering if I was in the mood for Chinese or something else, when it appeared.

The food truck.

I blinked.

It was still there, on the other side of the I-5 underpass, driving down Jackson toward me. Now it was coming closer, now it was turning onto a side street, now it was...parking? Really? I ran to the crosswalk and punched the button, then crossed even though the signal was still red. No one hit me.

The people around me had no idea what they were missing. I hurried past young professionals looking for an excellent dinner, immigrants with tired faces walking home from work, a rowdy group of Sounders fans clad in bright green matching shirts and celebrating a late-season soccer win. They all ignored the dark gray food truck and its promise of "THE BEST TERIYAKI IN SEATTLE," and I pitied them for it.

The sky darkened as I held my breath and turned the corner. It was still there.

It looked just as I remembered it, and he looked just as I remembered him. I stepped up confidently to the truck, wallet in hand, and greeted the tall, long-haired man.

"One order of spicy chicken teriyaki with brown rice," I said. "Also, a medium Coke and a side of gyoza."

"$8.50."

I paid with glee; I couldn't believe my luck. Inspired, I took out my iPhone and snapped a quick shot of the food truck to share with my fellow Chowhounds. Maybe someone would recognize it.

"You have returned," the man said as we waited for my meal.

"I've been looking for you guys for weeks," I said, fiddling with my phone. "From my perspective, you're the one who's returned."

"You're a connoisseur." He stroked his goatee.

"I do enjoy teriyaki. I make a living from it too, you know. I work at Uematsu House in Renton, if you're ever in the area."

"You understand the art. Rare."

"Sure, I guess. Some people wouldn't call it an art. Just food, to them. Whatever, they're wrong."

"We are cursed. The others are not."

"Their loss, as far as I'm concerned."

"I am cursed."

"So, like, do you come here often? Seriously, I've been looking for weeks. Do you guys use Twitter?"

"We are cursed to move from city to city, feeding the hungry and the damned, each of us unable to rest until men come to take our place on this vessel which has been forsaken by God."

The conversation had been going so well, too. Relatively. I stuck my iPhone back in my pocket and looked toward the museum.

"Do you often go there?" he asked.

"What?"

"The museum. Do you often visit?"

This was a strange topic. "Um, sure. I like art. I like seeing what local artists are doing, especially Asian-Americans. It makes me feel like I have a shot, too, you know?"

"Indeed."

"Besides, admission is free tonight."

"So I've heard."

"I like The Wing. It's kind of cozy, and I like the community focus. I like the other museums, too, though. Seattle Art Museum and whatever. I dunno. I guess it depends on my mood."

The bell chimed loudly. I thanked him and walked away, then turned to go back and ask if I could get an extra container of chili sauce. The truck was gone.

Shrugging, I hauled my loot to the small park on King and Maynard and sat across from a lonely old man playing a Chinese *erhu* on his knee. He sawed plaintively, his bow lurching between the two strings, his pentatonic tones lingering in the cold autumn air. I gave him some change. He asked me something in Mandarin.

"Sorry," I apologized.

"You are Chinese girl?" His accent was thicker than congee.

"Taiwanese."

"Chinese," he repeated. I let it slide.

The sauce had an extra sweet-sour tang I hadn't noticed before, maybe rice vinegar? There were subtle overtones of citrus, too, if I wasn't mistaken, possibly ponzu sauce. I crunched the deep-fried gyoza and licked the sauce off my chopsticks. The food truck was inching up on Ducky Teriyaki on my list. I'd need at least one more sample to know for sure. More than one. Probably several.

When I tried to upload the picture later, I couldn't find the file on my phone. I must have forgotten to save it.

7

I DIDN'T SEE THE teriyaki truck—or the guy—again for several weeks. The time passed slowly. I studied for midterms and drew portraits of Alice during the increasingly long lulls at Uematsu House. We put them on the walls in the dining area, replacing dusty pictures of cute puppies that had hung untouched for years.

"That one is cute," Alice said, pointing to a pencil drawing I'd just hung up. "I like the eyepatch."

Funny, I didn't remember putting an eyepatch on Alice, nor drawing that small pirate ship sailing away in the background.

Sam was back in town visiting Patrick. She must have felt guilty, though, because she invited us to brunch. "To welcome

Patrick to the family," she said. It was too little, too late.

We drove out together on Sunday, my parents and Sam and Patrick and I, to a reputable seafood place with a beautiful view of the water and an expensive buffet brunch.

Sam was in great spirits. She'd flown to California for two interviews already, including another interview with Natalie's firm, and she was expecting an offer in the next few days from a Bay Area firm in the Am Law 100. "Not as good as New York, of course," she said. "But definitely better than Seattle."

Somehow, Mom hadn't heard the news.

"San Francisco? You mean Seattle, no?"

"Mom, it's not set in stone yet. Patrick and I are still deciding where to live after the wedding. I can't quit my job until January anyway. I still have some matters to conclude."

"Samantha, I thought you were coming home to Seattle."

"We were thinking about it, but it wasn't the only option, okay? Patrick has a great opportunity at a startup with his old college friend in Emeryville. We're trying to keep our options open."

"But Samantha, you said you were coming back to Seattle. How can we be a family if you keep leaving?"

"Mom, you don't understand. There are many more legal opportunities in San Francisco."

I went back to the buffet for a new plate. Mom was a rock and Sam was a hard place, and I didn't want to get between them. Dad joined me a moment later, having excused himself as well.

"Did you know about San Francisco?" I asked.

"No, but it's Samantha's life. She has to make her own decisions. Did you try the crab?"

"Yes. I like it almost as much as the oysters. Did you try the French toast?"

"It was okay. Too sweet."

"Don't add so much maple syrup," I suggested. He laughed and returned to the table.

I was deciding what to dip next in the chocolate fountain when I heard Sam's voice, piercing, shrieking, through the restaurant.

"*I'm not perfect, okay?*" she screamed.

Oh crap. I didn't want to look. I focused on the buffet spread, deeply conscious that I was the only Asian-looking person in the buffet line. I took a wooden skewer and stabbed: Strawberry. Pineapple. Strawberry. Marshmallow. Banana. Pound cake. Strawberry.

"I could never please you. I tried so hard. I tried to be perfect, and it wasn't enough. It's never enough."

The fountain looked pretty good. I rotated my skewer in the languorous streams of chocolate, turning and shifting to thoroughly coat my delicious fruit kebab. One of the strawberries fell off, lost forever to the depths of the fountain's chocolatey abyss. I mourned its loss briefly, then stabbed a fresh victim onto the end of my spear.

"You want to take away the only thing that's mine, and I'm sick of it. I'm sick of being your daughter."

It was twenty-eight years of pent-up aggression exploding all at once. We should have foreseen it. We could have prevented it, let it out slow and steady like an overshaken can of soda, but we hadn't, and now Sam was having an extremely public breakdown in an extremely public place.

I peeked. Everyone around us pretended not to.

Mom's counter was predictable, routine, Sam's model for frosty. "Samantha, you're making a mistake. Listen to your mother. You're ruining your life."

"No, Mom, you're ruining my life. Patrick makes me feel happy and loved, unlike you."

Patrick, futile: "Sam—"

Sam stood up, grabbed her jacket. I didn't know what to do. She was hurting; she was stuck. We'd taken one car. Patrick looked worried. Dad looked concerned. The other diners looked away, embarrassed, except for a young girl who couldn't stop staring.

There was no other choice. I threw myself on the bomb, hoping to absorb the shrapnel. "Mom, Dad, I'm quitting school." Deflecting for Sam, like I always did, reminding our parents that it could be worse—Sam could be *me*.

"What?"

"I want to draw." Defensive: "I'll keep working at Uematsu House while I develop my career. Webcomics are really popular right now. I just need to draw mine on a regular schedule. Maybe I can own a studio someday."

"Daisy, what the hell?" Sam gaped, her condescending sisterly disbelief obliterating her earlier maternal conflict.

"I thought you were going to major in graphic design. Your mom and I were going to help you with college." That was Dad. He sounded a little hurt.

"I don't need anyone's help. I can do this myself." Defiant. Crumbling. I could taste my family's disappointment, and I wanted to cry. I kept my chin up instead, daring anyone to contradict me.

"Are you crazy?" Sam asked.

"I can," I insisted.

"No you can't. Daisy, you don't have the discipline."

"I am disappointed in both of my daughters," Mom announced, tight-lipped and simmering. "I regret having both of you."

"Mei-Fung," Dad cautioned.

"Not this again," Sam said. I didn't hear the rest because I'd already left the restaurant.

The food truck was there, waiting, as if it knew I needed it. I'd already filled up on oysters but I ordered anyway, anything to distract me. Mr. Tall-and-Gaunt was there, of course, thankfully silent and dropping his cursed shtick. I felt his mournful gaze upon me as he handed me my food. There was an extra pint of green tea ice cream in my bag, courtesy of the house. It was delicious.

Patrick found me on a bench staring at the water. "Hey."

"Hey."

"We're ready to go."

"What happened?"

"Not much. Sam accused your parents of setting you up for failure by having too high expectations. Your mom started to argue, but your dad stopped her. Sam's cleaning up in the bathroom. They sent me to get you."

"Thanks, I guess."

"Do you want to talk about it?"

"I dunno." Patrick wasn't a natural empath, but I was glad for the effort. He could be a self-centered jerk sometimes, but now wasn't one of them.

"If you want, I can get you in touch with a friend of mine," Patrick said. "He does graphic design for a local copy shop. He could tell you more about it."

"Oh?"

"Yeah. Lots of customer orders, helping them lay out posters and newsletters, things like that." He paused. "He hates his job."

"Oh."

"Is that your truck?" I followed his look. To my surprise, the goth teriyaki truck was still there.

"Oh yeah. That's the truck I keep talking about. You should try it because I don't know when's the next time we'll see it. Um, unless you want some of mine." I offered him my picked-at chicken.

Patrick wrinkled his nose. "I'll get my own. Come on."

The strange man was still standing next to the dark gray truck. No one seemed to notice him. I guess the weather was better for clam chowder; the fish shack seemed to be doing well. We walked up to the truck and the man greeted us solemnly.

"Can I order a small chicken teriyaki to go? No rice."

"You may order what you like," the man replied.

Patrick made conversation as we waited. "So, what's your name?"

"Richard."

"Nice to meet you, Richard. I'm Patrick. This is Daisy."

We shook hands. I was surprised at Richard's warmth; I thought he'd be as cold as a corpse.

"Daisy tells me that you're really hard to find."

The man looked at Patrick like he was an idiot. "We are

cursed. I am cursed. The truck is cursed. We must drive from place to place, forever cursed."

"Is the food cursed? Since everything else is cursed?"

"The food is cursed."

"Does that mean we shouldn't eat it?" I asked.

"Only the damned can find us. Only the damned can enjoy the cursed food we serve from this vessel."

"Wait, so if I enjoy your food, does that means I'm damned?" Patrick asked.

"Only the damned can find us," he repeated.

Sam appeared then, spotting us by the truck as she left the restaurant. She ran to us.

"I thought you were full," she accused Patrick.

"We Stefanis have a second stomach exactly for these kinds of situations. Some call it a blessing. Some call it a curse."

Richard stepped back into the shadow of the truck, and we stood around and waited for the chime, awkward-like.

"Did this guy say he was cursed to you?" Sam asked.

"Yeah."

"I still don't understand what that means. I mean, really? Cursed?"

"It's just a shtick. I wouldn't worry about it, smoochie-poo. You're overanalyzing again."

The low bell rang, followed by a chirp from Sam's Blackberry.

Patrick poked through his bag as we walked back to rejoin my parents by the car. "Check it out," he said, handing me a punch card.

The card was matte black. It featured ten rows of ten silver stars, and the first star was already punched through. There was no business name, but there was a seven-digit phone number scrawled in slanted silver script below the punch-spots.

I flipped it over. The backside was blank.

Jealous: "He never gave *me* a card."

"I'm sure he'd give you one if you asked."

"You'd better put that away before Dad sees it," Sam warned, looking up from her smartphone.

Patrick nodded and took the card back. "How did he fit all those stars on that tiny card?"

"I don't know," I said. "What do you think of the food?"

"Being damned is tasty. Sam, do you want a bite?"

"No way." She shuddered.

"Is it 'THE BEST TERIYAKI IN SEATTLE'?"

"It's definitely a strong contender. I wonder if they ever come to Kirkland."

The ride home was uncomfortable. I moped around the house, avoiding my parents as much as I could, and then went upstairs to draw. I didn't want to talk to them, and they didn't want to talk to me. Our family was so dysfunctional.

At least I still had Uematsu House.

TERIYAKI-DO: THE WAY OF TERIYAKI
Review: Puyallup Fair

Pat and I Did the Puyallup.

There, I said it. I hate the slogan, but I love the fair, even if the prices and the crowds seem to go up every year. This is a food blog, so I'll skip everything but the food—but for the record, Adam Lambert was *fabulous*.

You can find teriyaki at the fair, although it is scarce. (You might not want to; fair teriyaki is hardly a fair fare affair.) Wok King Cliché stirs up their Americanized Chinese menu with an oversweetened chicken teriyaki with sauce and chicken that are both of dubious provenance. The generic booth with the bright "Teri-Yaki" banner is likewise Terri-Ble, no matter how much nonsensical kanji and hiragana they paint on their sign.

The only fair teriyaki worth eating isn't really teriyaki at all. Hold Me, Grill Me, Kiss Me offers a chicken-on-a-stick option with a soy-based teriyaki-like sauce. It's more like yakitori, but it is far superior to the teriyaki-in-name-only slop being slung at the other booths.

This year, Hold Me is located near the petting zoo. Sometimes, live chickens strut around outside, oblivious to the barbaric acts you're perpetrating on their deceased brethren. Chickens are kind of dumb, so it's not like they know or care, but it's kind of awkward, especially if you drop a chunk of meat around them. (Simple solution: Don't drop it. Just eat it.)

And now for something completely different.

Teriyakiphiles can skip the remainder of this post. We're going to talk about The Hungry Weatherman, a new weather-themed vendor whose teriyaki-free menu is too fun not to share.

First: The corn-nado, fresh-roasted corn on the cob, dipped and fried in cornbread batter and served with a side of spicy creamed corn. The effect is a-maize-ing.

Second: Cliff Massmallows, sticky cumulus clouds of white popcorn bound together with marshmallow fluff. The treats are as breezy as the UW meteorologist's weather blog posts.

Then—there is the funnel cloud. There were reports of real funnel clouds in Puyallup last year, swirling pre-tornadoes in the sky. The Hungry Weatherman represents them in food with a hacked-up cotton candy machine filled with hot oil, running cones around the edges to quickly collect thin strips of extruded funnel cake batter. The result is a hand-held lump of light, crispy, deep-fried goodness covered in a snow of powdered sugar and a sweet, gooey lemon curd with a tart streak like lightning.

Meteorological phenomena never tasted so good.

8

SOMETHING SERIous was going on at work the next day. Everyone was there when I came in after class—Uematsu-san and Jay, Alice, and all the rest. They were seated in the dining room, talking quietly, passing around a box of tissues. I tiptoed through the belled glass door.

"Good afternoon, Uematsu-san. What's going on?"

"Daisy-chan, I have some bad news."

Remember the increasingly long lulls? I thought we were just going through a rough patch, but it was worse than that. Uematsu House was losing money, had been losing money since the beginning of the year, and Uematsu-san was planning to sell the store.

"What?"

"I've been running this store for twenty years. I'm ready to retire." Uematsu-san looked relaxed, relieved to tell us the news. I felt betrayed.

"You can't leave." I couldn't believe it.

"Daisy-chan, of course I can," Uematsu-san replied gently. "This is my store. We are no longer making money, and my daughter needs me. She is going back to work, and I am going to move to Spokane to take care of my grandson. Of course, I will write references for all of you."

I looked around. I had no backup. Alice was sniffling under tissues; the dishwashers were talking quietly amongst themselves. Jay looked uncomfortable.

Frustrated: "Jay, what are you going to do? Alice? Aren't you guys going to do anything?"

"There's nothing to do, Daisy," Jay said. "Uematsu-san has already made up her mind, as only she can do. She owns the store."

"Great."

"Maybe you can go to school full-time. You've been saving money, yeah? You live with your parents?"

I didn't know how to answer him without screaming. He didn't know what I'd said at brunch. Instead, I breathed deeply and counted to ten. "What happened? I thought we were doing pretty well. We get good reviews online."

"Bad economy," Uematsu-san replied. "The new teriyaki place across the street has increased competition." Teriyaki Maru. Their yakisoba wasn't too bad, but I thought their teriyaki chicken was only so-so. People were probably eating there for the novelty.

"Ingredients are more expensive now," she continued. "Wu Family Farms has been charging higher prices because the cost of gasoline went up. Our butcher also had to increase prices."

"Isn't there anything I can do?" I asked. "I could design a coupon. Maybe that would help business."

"Daisy-chan, I am going to sell the store. I miss my daughter. I'm sorry. You've been a good employee. We will close at the end of December."

I sat down, head in my hands, mind spinning. There was no way my parents would let me drop out of school now, not without a real job and income. Uematsu House had been good to me and I couldn't process the news, couldn't believe that it was going to go away. I breathed again, deeply, asked, "Uematsu-san, I need to go. Is that okay?"

"Yes. We're going to close early today."

"Okay. I'll see you tomorrow."

The teriyaki truck was waiting for me across the street, next to the gas station, exactly where I'd thought I'd seen it so many weeks ago.

"Hello," he greeted.

"Richard, right?"

"Yes."

"Are you guys hiring?"

His eyes were so green. I'd missed it before, but I saw them now as he stared at me, bore deep into my own eyes. I gasped, looking back into his thin, not-unattractive face, watching the bright emeralds watching me.

He hesitated only a moment. "Men only."

"What! That's sexual discrimination." I was outraged. Today was not going well at all.

"We are not bound by the laws of mortal men."

"Hell yeah, you are. Let me see your food handler's license."

Richard shook his head. "This burden cannot be yours to bear. Only other men can take the place of the cursed ones who serve this vessel, and so release them from misery."

"Bullshit." I went around the corner and took down the truck's license plate number. "I'm calling the cops on you guys. Or the Department of Health. Someone."

"As you wish. You'll find that they cannot affect things outside the mortal plane."

"Okay, fine, whatever. Can I just get a spicy chicken teriyaki with brown rice?"

He didn't give me a punch card, either.

Later, on the phone, Sam told me to drop it, said she didn't think I should work for a food truck anyway. "Especially if you've never met the other employees. You don't know what kind of people they are and seriously, Daisy, that food truck is mega-sketchy. Like, seriously."

"Don't I have a case? The guy flat-out told me, men only, no women allowed. That's discrimination."

"Daisy, what do you want to happen? Do you want to work for a food truck? Really? You should be in school, working on your bachelor's degree."

"Where's your sense of injustice? I thought you'd totally be on my side."

"I would be, if the case were worth fighting. It's not. A food truck like that isn't going to have anything to offer except a job, and you don't want to work there with that creepy guy."

"Saaaaaam."

"Drop it. Daisy, you need to grow up and start doing something with your life. Why don't you move to San Francisco with Patrick and me? There are some really good schools in the Bay Area. You could even study art. You don't have to study graphic design, you know."

Huh. That was an idea.

I plugged in the license plate online anyway, hoping to get the business name from the vehicle registration file at the Washington State Department of Licensing. Record not found, of course. *Of course.*

That night, I dreamed I wore a flowing green dress, standing on a ship next to a tall, green-eyed man. I tasted salty seawater on my lips from the northwest wind, or maybe I tasted tears; it's hard to remember when you dream. I remember we spoke, but I don't remember what we spoke about. I awoke with a single memory of his low, raspy voice:

"You silly, silly girl."

9

"**D**AISY."

"What."

It was a few days before Halloween, and it was Sam, calling for yet another wedding-related favor. I was still mad at her about the whole food truck thing, but I took the call anyway. After all, she was my sister.

"I need you to get our invitations from Hilde."

"Can't Patrick go?"

"He's in San Francisco looking at apartments. Don't worry, he said he'd take care of mailing them this weekend." I saw myself at our dining table, stuffing and stamping boxes of envelopes without him, but I didn't say a thing.

I didn't make it to Hilde's office until Halloween. It was

Monday, and Capitol Hill was filled with enthusiastic revelers in outlandish costumes. To my astonishment, the truck was there, too. Richard stood outside it, near a group of young men in bright, tight superhero outfits.

I didn't want to go; I really didn't. I was still mad at him. But the teriyaki allure was just too strong, and I wanted to take pictures of the food for my blog review. All of my earlier shots had been too blurry to use.

He seemed surprised to see me.

"Large spicy chicken with brown rice," I said in my best Mom/Sam voice.

Richard nodded, reported the order, then moved back to stand next to the truck. I waited.

Simultaneously:

"Why do you keep eating here?"

"Why won't you hire me?"

I looked bewildered. He looked chagrined.

"Can I, like, at least meet your cook?" I asked.

"I am the cook."

"But you stand out here."

He shook his head. "I am the proprietor, the cook, the chef, the clerk, the waiter, the dishwasher. My crew is damned to carry out my orders, acting as mere extensions of me."

"Hmm. Hey, can I get a punch card?"

"There are none remaining to give."

"Really." I thought I saw a stack on the counter. He shifted his weight to block it.

"Look," I continued. "I just want to know where to find you. I mean, I don't agree with your hiring practices, and it sounds like you're kind of a tough manager, but your food's pretty good, and I appreciate that. It's hard to find really great teriyaki, if you know what I mean."

"I cannot know where next my crew will go."

"Fine, okay. You don't want me as a customer. Whatever."

Pause, then: "Yes. I do not want you as a customer."

This guy clearly didn't know how to run a business. I didn't know what he had against me, but it wasn't worth my time to figure it out. I didn't care if he *did* serve "THE BEST TERIYAKI IN SEATTLE."

"Fine."

The bell chimed.

I looked back as I paused outside the door to Sørensdóttir Event Services, clasping a plastic bag with the last serving of chicken teriyaki I'd ever get from that truck. He was still there, watching me with his sad, mournful eyes. I turned away to walk into the office.

"What is that disgusting smell?"

I sniffed and held up my bag. "This?"

Hilde filled the doorway, her large bulk barring me from entry. "Get rid of it."

"What? You can't be serious."

"Do not bring that filth inside."

"What are you talking about? It's just teriyaki."

"It is filth. Do not bring it into my domain."

"Fine." I grumbled, then set my untouched bag on the ground next to the door. She relaxed slightly and led me inside.

"Sam wants me to pick up the invitations."

"Wait here."

The office hadn't changed in the weeks since I'd last visited. Hilde still had a desk, bookshelves, and two breathtaking pieces of totally un-wedding-appropriate art on her walls.

Well... One of the books looked disturbed. The scarlet one.

I listened; I heard no footsteps. Holding my breath, I moved quietly to the bookshelf and leaned down.

I touched the book and began to pull it out. The scarlet leather binding was soft, almost velvety. I felt the gilded vines as bumps under my fingers, shallow texture on the thick volume. The vines continued along the front and back covers. Slowly, gently...

"What are you doing?" yelled a loud, familiar voice.

I jumped. I didn't think people did that in real life, but apparently they do. The cower was also inevitable. I was helpless.

Loud footsteps—where did she come from? I should have heard her approaching from the hall outside her office; the wooden floors should have given her away. I felt the weight of her presence behind me, glaring at me through the back of my head. I cringed.

"I suggest you put that back."

I shivered.

I shoved the book back into its place on the shelf, stood up, put my hands in my pockets, and rushed back to my chair. Even as my stomach betrayed me, I faked nonchalance: "Oh, hi. Did you get the invitations?"

Hilde ignored me, dropping boxes onto the table and kneeling with surprising grace to pull the book out and inspect it. She touched the cover gently with long, red-manicured fingers as her face flipped from rage to concern. I felt guilt wash over me, and I hoped I hadn't damaged something which was precious to her.

She returned the book to the shelf, and rage returned to her face. "Do not ever touch my possessions again."

"Um, okay."

"If I catch your grubby little fingers on my precious, beautiful things, I will destroy you so fast, it will seem that you had never existed."

"Hey, I'm sorry, I didn't mean—"

"Your entire family will feel my wrath. I will hunt down your parents. I will sabotage your sister's wedding."

"Look, there's no reason to—"

"You do not understand." Hilde was almost on top of me now, her face inches from mine. I slid lower in the chair.

"I understand. I was just—"

"Let me repeat. You. Do. Not. Understand." Her breath smelled like sardines. I wondered if she owned cats. She could totally be a crazy cat lady.

"Yes," I squeaked.

"These books are my things. They belong to me. They are my dearest possessions. You are nothing compared to these books."

I nodded, unable to speak.

She motioned brusquely at the boxes. "Take these and begone. Never come here again. You are banned from my abode."

I took the invitations and gratefully slunk away, calling Sam as soon as I got to the car.

"Daisy, what? I'm at work."

"Your wedding planner is *crazy*! Where did you find this woman?"

"Did you touch her books?"

"She made me feel like a criminal. Geez. I was just looking."

"You need to learn to respect other people's property."

"She made me get rid of my teriyaki, too. Crap." I'd left it in front of the office. I dashed out of the car, ignoring Sam's questions in my ear, hoping my bag would still be there untouched.

It was gone. I swore.

"Call me later," Sam said, then hung up.

True to his word, Patrick came over early on Friday night to help prepare the invitations.

"Hello, Mrs. Wang," Patrick said, grinning from the front door. He sounded cheerful.

Mom ignored him and turned around. He followed.

I'd laid the invitations out on the dining table. Sam had insisted that we glue a lace border onto each one. I didn't think she'd know if we skipped them, but despite her misgivings about the upcoming nuptials, Mom insisted that we honor Sam's request.

Patrick sat down next to me and immediately fell into a lace-gluing routine. Mom was stuffing finished invitations into envelopes.

"Mom, did you print the address labels?"

"No. The printer would not work. I hate this computer."

Patrick looked up. "Can I help?"

"Patrick's good with computers," I said. "Give him a chance."

Mom nodded, tight-lipped. Patrick followed her into the den.

It was just me, two boxes of invitations, two pairs of scissors, three sticks of glue, and six rolls of lace. I sighed, gluing.

I'd looked up Sørensdóttir Event Services after the incident with Hilde. Internet reviews were mixed. There were many one-star reviews from vendors with grudges, people who had been put out of business by Hilde because of some real or perceived slight during the wedding process. There were a few glowing reviews from happy brides waxing narcissistic about their perfect days.

There were several middle-of-the-pack reviews, including one or two emphasizing her aggressive personality. These were the most interesting.

"She gets the wedding done, no matter what," read one. "Even if you realize that you don't actually want to get married."

"She used to be engaged," read another. "But her own wedding was ruined when a bad vendor changed the catering order and sent the groom into a lethal anaphylactic shock. That's why she's so tough."

Mom returned with a stack of address stickers.

"Did he fix it?" I asked.

"Yes," she begrudged. She set the stickers down and resumed stuffing envelopes. A few minutes later, Patrick came back to help.

The glue sticks were inadequate and the lace was too thin. I re-rubbed adhesive with my thumb, trying not to tear anything.

Patrick passed a finished invitation to Mom. She took it without comment.

I tore a bit of lace and suppressed an impolite word. Sam

would never see it. I smoothed it over the glue to straighten it out, and I passed the finished product to Mom.

"Mrs. Wang?"

Mom ignored him. He shrugged.

Patrick was outpacing me. I paused to study his technique. Instead of cutting four separate pieces of lace, he was slicking glue quickly along the outside of the invitation, then laying a single stream of lace atop it and folding over the corners. He was introducing a little bit of skew, but if it was good enough for the groom, it was good enough for me.

"Hey Pat, want to get lunch tomorrow?" I asked. "There's a new teriyaki place in the U District."

"Sorry, Daisy." Strange. Patrick didn't usually turn down my lunch invitations.

Patrick's technique really was more efficient. I polished off another invitation and put it in Mom's stack.

"Richard has ruined me for anyone else," he added. "I don't think I'll ever eat at another teriyaki place again."

I stopped in mid-glue. "What?"

"Richard? The guy with the teriyaki truck? You introduced us a few weeks ago."

"You've been eating there?"

"All the time. The food is perfect. The more I taste, the more I realize just how perfect it is. Everything else pales in comparison." He finished lacing another invitation.

"I know that." I suppressed a surge of jealousy and resumed gluing, pressing *extra hard* on the invitations. Mom was applying address labels to envelopes, ignoring us.

"I can't find the truck," I added. "Besides, he doesn't want to sell teriyaki to me. He told me so." Jerkface.

"Daisy, you don't find the truck. You call the truck." Patrick stopped gluing, fumbling in his pocket. I took advantage of the pause to catch up.

"Here. You just call him." Patrick handed me the unmarked black punch card. He'd already filled out three rows of stars.

"Really?"

"Yeah. He usually answers right away. Do you want a pen?"

"Sure. Thanks." I scribbled the phone number on the side of a box and handed the card back to him.

Patrick was almost done with his stack of invitations. I gave him some of mine.

Dad came in from the living room. He and Mom conversed briefly in Taiwanese, but I wasn't quick enough to understand it, something about the k-drama, I think. Last I heard, Eun-Mi's long-lost sister, who was deeply religious, had appeared with a priest to exorcise the evil spirit from Jung-Hoon's body.

"What's going on?"

"The spirit was removed from Jung-Hoon's body, but the priest could not get rid of it," Dad explained. "Now it is in Eun-Mi's womb."

"Oh."

"Jung-Hee still does not know about the evil spirit. He is planning to kill himself so his wife can live with his brother."

"That's not good."

"He told Jung-Hoon already. Jung-Hoon was going to stop him, but he is in a coma from the ritual. Eun-Mi's sister is taking care of him."

The story was getting too complicated to follow. I sighed and kept gluing.

Dad joined us, sitting next to Mom and pasting stamps. Sam had insisted on a special design, a silver monogram joining the letters "S" and "P", and the stamps came non-adhesive. I handed him a gluestick so he could spare his taste buds.

Abruptly: "Mrs. Wang, why do you dislike me so much?"

My jaw dropped. Patrick was blunt, but this was unprecedented.

"I don't mean to be rude, but the wedding is in a month. We really need to talk about it. I know it's bothering Sam, and it's really bothering me. I'm not going to join a family where I'm not welcome."

Mom's face was tight-lipped disapproval. Like always.

Dad touched her arm. "Mei-Fung, let us listen to Patrick. Samantha is going to marry him. The wedding should be a happy occasion."

"He did not ask," she burst.

I was astonished. "Patrick, you didn't ask?" We'd been trained, hard. One of our cousins had been disowned because her now-husband hadn't asked my aunt and uncle for permission before he proposed. Sam would have prepped Patrick if she thought marriage was even a remote possibility.

Patrick and Dad looked at each other. Guiltily. Hmm.

"Mei-Fung, Patrick asked me," Dad said. "We did not want to tell you because we thought you would spoil the surprise for Sam." I'd never seen my mom so speechless.

"It is my fault because I did not tell you," he continued. "I'm sorry."

"Kai-Yuen, I would not tell," she protested. This was probably true; it's not like Sam and Mom ever talked to each other. Still, I could see their point.

"We could not take the chance."

"You can trust me."

"Mei-Fung, you told Mei-Ling about George's new job when George made a special dinner so he could tell her by himself. You told Siao-Yue's husband about the divorce before she could talk about it with him. You told Ya-Cin about Geng-Hao's affair with Sally. You are too nosy."

"I would not tell," she insisted. "Besides, Patrick will not understand Sam. They do not have the same culture. They cannot get married."

"Sam and I have a lot in common," Patrick said. "I'm sorry you don't see it, but it's true. We do have our differences. But that means we've got a lot to share with each other."

"It is no good." But I saw Mom waver briefly.

Patrick hadn't won this battle, but armed with his new intelligence, maybe he could win the war. Besides, Dad and I were on his side.

TERIYAKI-DO: THE WAY OF TERIYAKI

Review: Teriyaki Yurt

This place makes me cringe. It's not because the food is bad or because the service sucks; in fact, both the food and the service are passable. It's not because of the location, though parking can be difficult on the weekends. No, Teriyaki Yurt makes me cringe because it's too cutesy for its own good.

Let's start with the name. Yurt? Really? Teriyaki Yurt? When Pat told me about this place, I couldn't believe it. I was, like, "What the hell is a yurt?" Apparently I don't go camping enough. Pat says the Washington State Park System is full of rentable yurts, mimicking the warm portable dwellings that were once used by Mongolian nomads.

Okay, fine, Mongolian makes sense then, because Teriyaki Yurt isn't really a teriyaki place—it's an all-you-can-eat Mongolian barbecue place with a decent teriyaki sauce (and a decent ginger sauce, and a decent sweet and sour sauce, and...). Except, Mongolian barbecue isn't really Mongolian, and I'm still not sure what the "teriyaki" part buys them, but, sure, whatever, let's go with it. Like Pat says, just suspend your disbelief.

From the outside, it is squat and round and actually does look like a yurt. It's also across the street from two other teriyaki shops (Teriyaki Snap! and Minna Teriyaki). Inside, you'll find large furs hanging on the walls and strewn along the bare cement floor. The waitstaff, clad in burly garments, will direct you to rustic tables and answer you only in short, mumbling grunts. Your water glass will probably be dirty, and there will be no ice. You'll hear stylized oriental music being played on a short loop in the background.

Not cutesy enough? The buffet line will be crowded. You'll be handed one large bowl (chipped) for your meats and vegetables, one small bowl (also chipped) for your sauce. At the grill, you'll meet a chef with an eyepatch and a big cleaver, who will scream and shout unintelligible syllables as he flourishes his (largely decorative) knife dramatically above your swiftly cooking food. Sometimes, the chef will get carried away, and you'll be left with mush instead of meal because he pulverizes the ingredients.

Last time I came here, I tried making a meal purely of chicken teriyaki. First, I selected the best-looking pieces of raw chicken from the buffet and brought them to the grill with only teriyaki sauce. Then, I selected the best-looking pieces of broccoli, cauliflower, onion, and carrot, and brought them (along with more teriyaki sauce) to get cooked on the side. The results were okay, though I do think the chef engaged in more flourishing than was strictly necessary.

I wouldn't really come here for teriyaki. I'd come here for the theatrics and the beef, which is usually sliced pretty thin and tastes pretty good when grilled with the fat green tea noodles. Tastes will vary on the sauce, but I like to use a thirty/seventy mix of chili garlic sauce and honey-ginger. Pat's a fan of the orange chili oil. Just remember to check your eyerolls at the door, or get your food to go.

10

LIFE AT UEMATSU House never returned to normal after Uematsu-san's announcement. It was hard to care when you knew you were getting shut down soon. We kept a calendar on the wall and Xed our way through it as the weather turned cold.

It was the weekend before Thanksgiving and the store was dead. Alice had taken the week off, so Jay and I were the only staffers at the restaurant. I was sketching. He posed patiently, one knife poised over a half-cut onion as I practiced capturing the scene on paper.

"Turn the blade toward me, please." He obliged.

"Jay, what are you going to do when Uematsu-san closes the store?"

"I'll find another job, just like I did before and just like I'll do again."

"That's a good attitude."

"Maybe I'll ask the new owners for a job," he said.

"Did someone buy the store?"

"Not yet. She had one offer but it fell through."

"That's too bad." My onion looked a little square. I rounded the edges to plump it up.

"What if the new owners are bad?" I asked. "I'd hate to work at a place like Kawaii Bento. I don't know what they put in the sauce, but it's totally gross."

"Sometimes you gotta help other people see how to get there. But sometimes, a job's just a job."

I nodded.

"What about you? School?" Jay asked.

"I guess. Sam said I could stay with her and Patrick in San Francisco. I've been doing a little research. Maybe I can get an art history degree and be a curator."

"Yeah."

My knife wasn't sharp enough. I emphasized the line of the blade, softened the handle for contrast.

"How's your daughter?"

"She wants to start dating boys. I told her she's too young."

"She's not that young. She's in high school, right?"

"She's only fourteen."

"I started dating when I was fourteen." Jeremy, my first crush. We'd dyed identical Converse knockoffs for Twin Tolo, but my shoes weren't dry and I bled blue all over my lucky socks. Last I checked, Jeremy was practicing real estate in Los Angeles.

"I'm just trying to protect her. I don't want anyone to break her heart."

"You have to let her grow up sometime, Jay."

"Are you seeing anyone?"

"No," I replied, thinking of goth teriyaki trucks.

"That's too bad. You're a nice kid. Maybe you should find a nice boy and settle down."

"Ugh, no way." Domesticity was most definitely not for me.

I drove home tired, but seeing Patrick's BMW in our driveway jolted me awake.

"Hi Daisy," he called from the dining room.

Most of the dinner spread was already gone—stir-fried shrimp with egg and peas, short ribs braised with garlic and soy sauce, a large plate of watercress, a small bowl of spicy-sweet pickled cucumber slices. My parents and Patrick were sitting around looking like thieves after an art heist. Patrick appeared to be on his third bowl of rice. I pulled up a chair to observe this new family dynamic.

"Patrick came to bring the favors for the wedding," Mom said. "Because he was so nice, we asked if he wanted to have dinner with us."

"Mei-Fung is an awesome cook, Daisy." He grabbed the last short rib with his chopsticks. I almost killed him.

"Patrick said he would show me how to create an account on Facebook," Mom said. "Then we can keep in touch with Sam when she moves to San Francisco." I foresaw Sam and myself competing to cause Patrick's death.

"Dad, did your TV show end yet?" I asked as I beat Patrick to the last piece of shrimp.

"The last episode is tonight."

Dad and I left Patrick in the kitchen with Mom. I didn't know what was going on, but I didn't mind if he wanted to wash the dishes.

"Dad." I wasn't sure how to tell him. "Mrs. Uematsu is closing the store. She told us a few weeks ago. I'll be unemployed soon."

"What are you going to do, Daisy?"

"I don't know. Sam says I could move to San Francisco with her. There are some really good schools down there." I hesitated. "I don't know if I can pay for tuition."

"Daisy, you know that your mom and I will pay for school."

"I don't know. I haven't applied anywhere yet. I don't want to study a trade, though. I want to study art, like real art. Maybe art history."

Dad sat back. I couldn't read him at all.

"I could become a curator or maybe an appraiser."

He wasn't buying it. I slumped.

"Daisy, you need to think about what will be the best career for you. Your mom and I are happy to pay for that degree if you can really make a job from it."

"Okay. I might look for another restaurant job, too." I wished again that Uematsu-san wouldn't close the store.

We switched on the TV to find Jung-Hoon still comatose in bed as Eun-Kyung, Eun-Mi's sister, prayed next to him. Mom joined us as we watched Jung-Hee stand alone in a room, contemplating a gun and talking to himself. I could hear Patrick loading the dishwasher.

Eun-Mi was going into labor and the only one around was the priest. I decided to join Patrick in the kitchen.

"How was San Francisco? Did you find an apartment?"

"Apartment?"

"Sam said you were in San Francisco looking at apartments. That's why I had to pick up the invitations. Your wedding planner is crazy, by the way."

"I know." He turned off the water.

"So? Where are we living? I hear SoMa's pretty cool."

Patrick was moving some plates around to make space on the bottom rack. "We?"

"Sam said I could live with you guys if I went to school in San Francisco."

"Did she?" He knocked over some silverware. I heard the forks clatter on the floor and went over to help pick them up.

"Yeah. I can, can't I? I was thinking, maybe the change of environment would make it easier to go to school."

Patrick was quiet. He was making me nervous.

"I know I annoy you guys sometimes, but I could get a job. I could pay a little rent. I probably can't afford my own apartment though. San Francisco is pretty expensive."

"Well, Daisy." Patrick straightened up. "There's a complication."

"Oh yeah?"

"Yeah." Patrick turned on the sink and began rinsing the next stack of dishes.

"What's the complication?"

"Diego's startup imploded. His biz dev guy started sleeping with one of the venture capital folks."

"Uh oh."

"Well, that could have been okay, but then they hired his ex-girlfriend to run UX. And then, it turns out the VC was married, and her husband found out, and now they've lost their funding. It's all falling apart."

"Wow."

"Yeah. Sam was right. You shouldn't mix business with friendship. I'm glad I didn't quit my job here." He ran water over Mom's favorite serving platter, scrubbing gently with a yellow sponge.

"No kidding. Did Sam say she told you so?"

Patrick shook his head. "I haven't told her yet."

"But you're going to tell her, right?"

"Daisy, she really wanted to move to San Francisco. I'm looking for other jobs. I'll find something else, then I'll tell her."

"Pat." This could only lead to trouble.

"Don't worry. People are always hiring programmers."

"You have to tell her."

"In fact, I have an interview next week."

"Pat, it's important."

"I'll tell her after the interview. It'll be easier if I already have another job lined up."

"Promise?"

"Daisy, don't worry. I'm not an idiot." He handed me the platter.

"Okay." I stuck it in the dishwasher and watched him wash another plate.

Casually: "Hey, are you still eating at that teriyaki truck?"

"Richard's truck?"

"Yeah. The weird one with the pirate logo."

He nodded, handed me a wet serving spoon. "I had it for lunch yesterday. And today."

"Oh." I tried not to bend the spoon.

"I gave you the number, right?"

"Yeah. No one ever picks up." Or calls back when I leave a voicemail. Jerk.

"That's weird. Want me to call right now?"

"No. I don't care."

"Up to you." He shrugged, then shut off the water.

Back in the living room, Jung-Hoon had woken up and declared his love for Eun-Kyung, who had waited so patiently beside him, then stopped his older brother Jung-Hee before he pulled the trigger on himself. The brothers and Eun-Kyung were now racing to find Eun-Mi, who was still in labor with a priest for a midwife.

We watched as the priest raised his arms in the air, beseeching a higher power to remove the demonic spirit from the baby. There was a flash, then a baby's cry. Jung-Hee ran into the room, followed by the others.

"Jung-Hee," she called.

"Eun-Mi," he replied, cradling his wife in his arms.

Beside them, Eun-Kyung took the newborn from the priest and swaddled it, then handed the baby to her sister. Jung-Hoon embraced her and asked the priest to marry them on the spot.

A happy ending—or was it? The bright noise of the joyous scene faded away, and the camera panned to the baby's squalling face. Its eyes glowed red.

II

IT WAS TEN DAYS before the wedding, then seven, then five, then three. Sam took vacation time from work and flew back early for wedding preparations. She kept us busy, making us put flags with names and table assignments into chocolate truffles, or glue dried flower petals onto guest name badges.

"I have to study for finals," I lied, escaping.

Really, I needed an art pick-me-up. I hadn't been to the Seattle Asian Art Museum in a while, so I headed to Volunteer Park, hoping for inspiration. Sam would never know.

The park was gorgeous, even though it was cold. I patted a stone camel on the nose on my way into the building, looking forward to the special exhibit, "Demons in Asian Culture." The first room featured examples in Japanese art—painted and constructed representations of demons and spirits from Japanese folklore.

Invariably, I was reminded of Uematsu House. Uematsu-san was closing the store in less than a month, and no one had stepped up to buy the restaurant. Jay was job hunting in earnest. Alice was preparing to move to Spokane and lamenting all the Mariners games she would miss in the spring. I was depressed and undecided, on a trajectory for full-time classes during winter quarter at the community college. I didn't want to go, but I couldn't justify not going. I knew my parents would be disappointed if I didn't.

I stood admiring a red/gold oni mask when I suddenly felt myself being watched.

I turned around and did a double take. It was Richard.

He looked so vulnerable without the goth truck behind him. I wondered what he was doing here. Admiring a woodblock print by Utamaro, apparently.

He saw that I saw, and he stepped forward. "Daisy."

I nodded coldly.

He didn't seem to have anything else to say. I looked at him for a moment, then turned back to the mask. Between red puffed cheeks, the mask bore a huge, evil grin which I found rather unsettling.

I shook my head and moved on to the next piece. Richard followed me.

"Do you like art?" I asked.

"I have long been the acquaintance of many artists."

"This museum must seem quite foreign to you. After all, Asian cultures are so exotic."

"No more so than others."

I observed a piece of glazed earthenware from the Ming dynasty, a beast-headed humanoid which the gallery described as an officer of hell. Near it was a brightly painted Chinese hell scroll depicting a scene in one of the earlier courts.

"Where's your truck?"

"Elsewhere."

The detail was admirable, but the scene was horrific. I moved on quickly to a Tibetan thangka featuring two hideous demons cavorting in a cluster of embroidered limbs. I winced.

"Patrick is your friend," he said.

"He's my sister's fiancé. They're getting married this weekend."

"You care about him."

"He's a good guy. I'm glad he's joining the family. He's the best boyfriend Sam's ever had."

"He eats too much teriyaki."

I laughed. "Patrick doesn't eat as much teriyaki as I do."

"His time draws near. He must not permit his gluttony to overcome his judgment."

"Why do you care? I'm sure you're making good business off him."

"I did not come for his sake."

This guy didn't make any sense. "If you think he's eating too much food, why don't you stop selling it? He said you show up whenever he wants."

"I am compelled to answer his calls."

"Why don't you answer when I call? It always goes to voicemail."

"I'm quite busy," he said. At least he had the decency to look slightly embarrassed.

I glared at him and moved forward to examine a Burmese ceramic tile featuring donkey-headed demons from a Buddhist story.

Apropos of nothing, I heard him cry: "Would that I could be rid of this damned curse!"

"Huh?"

He didn't answer. I shrugged and headed into the next room. Sam would have pressed, but I wasn't my sister.

Okay, maybe I was a little curious.

"You're not really cursed. Not like this." I motioned at the gallery walls, at all of the demons surrounding us.

"No, it is so." He looked glum.

"Um, so, like, you're a demon or a ghost or something?"

"I am the captain of an accursed crew, forever doomed to an eternity of restlessness, luring gluttons to join us through the siren tastes of their final meals."

Awkward.

"Truly, we serve 'THE BEST TERIYAKI IN SEATTLE' for did we not, none would return to claim his infernal fate, and so release one of my crew members from his own lifeless existence."

"I still don't get it. Sorry."

"As well you shouldn't, for you are mortal, and none can grasp the position of the damned until he himself occupies it."

Whatever, sure, I could play along. "Well, can't you get rid of the curse, or whatever?"

Richard shook his head. "I cannot say because I do not

know. I made a terrible mistake once, and this curse is my punishment. I doubt it can be broken."

"What did you do?"

He looked pained. "I did not understand love, and so I broke a commitment I did not take seriously. Through my actions, two lovers became separated by death. I had not realized the power of true affection, until that moment."

"Oh." I didn't feel particularly enlightened.

"I must go. I've said too much."

"Um, okay." Pause. "Can I see you again?"

"That would be unwise." He gave me a quick half-bow, then disappeared behind a corner. I tried to follow, but he was already gone.

TERIYAKI-DO: THE WAY OF TERIYAKI
Review: Rotisserie Princess

I love Rotisserie Princess. I love everything about it—I love the tall rotisserie machines, turning, basting, and injecting chicken in five different flavors (including Chipotle Fire and Honey-Sesame Teriyaki). I love the perky-happy restaurant staff, who are more cheerful than anyone has any right to be, working minimum wage at a franchise. I love the TV commercials featuring Chloë Clucker, the Rotisserie Princess herself, donning her Rotisserie crown of jewels (each gemstone representing a classic RP flavor, including an opal for the now-defunct Pineapple Paradise).

Pat doesn't like the gimmick, but even he admits that it is awe-inspiring to walk through the door of a Rotisserie Princess.

It's a bit like watching the donut machines at Krispy Kreme. At Rotisserie Princess, though, you don't get conveyor belts taking donuts on their epic journeys from flour to tasty. Instead, you get a bank of glass cabinets, each enclosing a rotating vertical spit with rotating prongs stuck with whole chickens, as if some hellish alien robot has whirred its way through a chicken coop and stabbed its numerous angled arms into the hapless denizens within.

Large brushes surround the vertical spit, continuously spreading fresh coats of sauce onto the cooking chickens, becoming a sauce-filled chicken carwash of deliciousness. I could watch the chickens for hours. And often, I do—the lines are *slow* (another Pat criticism). The one near my house is always packed with unhurried senior citizens, bored high school kids, impatient families with small screaming toddlers in paper Rotisserie crowns, tapping on the glass like fish tanks. The chickens keep turning, oblivious, until finally the door is opened and a smiling Rotisserie Maid or Squire captures the roasted beasts with tongs, filling wide metal trays as the smell of just-charred flesh overwhelms the store.

I think it's worth the wait. Like I said, Pat disagrees, though he never turns down splitting a three-pounder with me. He's not a rotisserie fan anyway—he prefers real grilled teriyaki to roasted chicken with teriyaki glaze. I understand his point, but I don't care. As a loyal subject, I raise my plastic soda cup high and proudly toast my regent. Long may the Rotisserie Princess reign.

12

DECEMBER THIRD, the day of the wedding. Mom woke me up too early; our hair appointment wasn't until nine-thirty and the ceremony wasn't until three o'clock in the afternoon.

"We must pick up the decorations," she insisted.

"Sam said Hilde's taking care of that." I rolled over and covered myself with a blanket. I'd been up late counting wedding favors, and I was feeling grumpy.

I found myself driving to the site with a full carload of wedding-related junk for company. Sam and Patrick had picked a former millionaire's mansion on Lake Washington, a large, lofty place that hadn't seen residential use since the end of the tech bubble. It was gray outside, freezing cold and threatening to rain, but the hedges were well-trimmed and the mansion was grand. I hoped the weather would improve (it didn't) and was glad that I'd decided to bring my bridesmaid's dress rather than wear it.

"Hey, Daisy." I found Patrick first, wearing shorts and flip-flops and a tattered black *Pirates of the Caribbean* movie shirt. He stood beside an attractive couple in front of the house. Patrick was shivering, and I wasn't sure if it was due to his outfit or his nerves.

"Pat, you're wearing that? In this weather?"

"I ran out of laundry. I've been a little busy."

He shrugged, then turned to motion to his companions. "Daisy, this is Diego, my best man, and his girlfriend, Rebecca. Daisy is Sam's younger sister."

We shook hands. Diego was long-haired and lean; Rebecca was cute and curvy. They smiled broadly with blindingly white teeth.

"We met at the rehearsal dinner," Diego said.

"You're the one with the startup, right?"

"Not any more. We lost our funding."

"Oh yeah." Remembering, I asked, "Pat, did you ever find another job?"

Patrick shook his head. "I'm still looking. I have another phone interview next week."

"Oh, okay. Good luck."

Sam and Patrick must have decided that he could be unemployed for a few months. It's not like Sam wasn't making twice his salary anyway.

My future brother-in-law fidgeted, rubbing his arms and shoulders for warmth.

"Nervous?" I asked.

"Yeah. I'm thinking about calling Richard."

"You're still eating there?"

"You bet. There's no way I could've made it this far without him. Check it out."

Patrick fished around for his wallet, then pulled out a familiar black card with silver stars. "Only one punch to go."

I did a quick calculation—seven weeks since the restaurant fight, ninety-nine punches on the card...

"You've been eating there twice a day? No wonder you're getting chubby." Richard was right; Patrick *was* eating too much teriyaki.

"I still fit in my tux." He sounded a little defensive.

"What are you guys talking about?" Rebecca asked.

"Oh, Daisy found this food truck that serves excellent chicken teriyaki. It's total crack. You guys should try it."

"You said you just call?"

"Yeah, the guy usually shows up right away. Great customer service. He's a little weird, though."

Oh, right. "Hey, I saw Richard—"

"Daisy!" It was Sam, coming around the corner, calling for me. "Where are you?"

Patrick blanched. "I'd better go. She doesn't want us to see each other before the ceremony. Diego, want to see the pond?"

"Sure."

"Talk to you later, Daisy."

"Nice to meet you," added Rebecca as they headed away from the house.

Sam appeared, dressed casually in a dark red turtleneck over jeans. "There you are. Do you have the vases?"

"They're in my car."

"Okay, good. Go find Hilde. She's in the ballroom. The florist needs the vases so we can set up the tables."

Hilde? I hadn't seen her since that thing with the book on Halloween, and I was really hoping to avoid her. Which, come to think of it, was maybe a little unrealistic, given that she was kind of running the wedding.

"Um, shoot. Sam, I told Mom I could pick up Great-Aunt Jade." Technically true; Mom had asked me before she found out that Great-Aunt already had a ride.

"I have to go now," I added. "You guys can get the vases later. Promise."

Sam gave me her very best death glare. "Daisy, Great-Aunt Jade is already here. She's gnawing on appetizers at the bar. Stop making excuses."

Panic: "Sam, I can't go. Hilde hates me. Besides, I don't want to get her crazy on me."

"Oh, Daisy, she doesn't hate you. Just go inside."

Shaking her head, Sam propelled me toward the entrance. I gave her a wild look as the doors shut between us.

"See you later," she called.

The entry was large, but I wouldn't have expected less from a mansion. I slunk past a sparkling chandelier and gold-framed portraits of people I didn't know, then entered the ballroom, hoping Hilde wasn't there.

She was. She saw me immediately. My stomach fell.

Hilde was dressed for battle in a scarlet pantsuit with her golden pigtails tied neatly behind her, and armed with a clipboard and several red pens. She was followed by two women in dark suits wearing earbuds and looking professional. I wondered where they kept their sunglasses.

"Where are the vases?" she demanded.

"In the car."

"Where is the car?"

"Outside."

She stared. "Of course the car is outside, you fool."

I bit my tongue, resisting the urge to talk back. Irrationally, I was struck by the image of Hilde in a shining Viking hat, singing melodramatic Wagnerian arias and drinking from a beer horn as she chased me down astride a large white horse.

"Give me your keys," she demanded suddenly.

"What?" Indignant.

"You are not reliable. Doris will retrieve the vases." One of the two assistants stepped forward and held a palm out expectantly.

"That's outrageous. Look, I'll just go run and get my car. I'll be back in a few minutes. Meet you guys outside the lobby."

"Doris, follow her." I glared at the wedding planner, but I didn't protest.

As soon as we were out of earshot, I asked, "So, what's it like to work for Hilde? Is it true she once drowned a litter of Dalmatians because she thought the furs would look good on the bride?"

No response.

"I heard that one time, she chased down a runaway groom across state lines. On *foot*. And then she knocked him unconscious, threw him over her shoulder, and ran him back to the bride, and they *still* started the reception ten minutes early."

I glanced back at Doris. Her face was still blank.

"This other time, I heard that Hilde and the mother of the bride got into such a *huge* argument that they took it outside to the chapel graveyard, and Hilde *dominated* her in total ninjitsu hand-to-hand combat *during the ceremony*, and no one noticed a thing. The bride? Chuck Norris's sister. That's right, Hilde beat up *Chuck Norris's mom*."

I caught a shadow of a smirk. I grinned back and unlocked my car. "Jump inside."

"The last one is true," Doris said. "I was there. Chuck Norris's mom was being a total bitch."

My jaw dropped. "Chuck Norris has a sister?"

"Hell if I know."

She buckled up. I handed her the box she'd displaced and started the engine.

"Hilde is a strange person," she began.

"You don't say."

"I've never met someone so committed to a cause. She's practically Cupid. Couples *must* fall in love. Couples *must* get married. Once Hilde has decided that you belong together, she'll make sure you stay together. She only accepts clients when she thinks the couple is a true match, whatever that means."

"That's crazy," I said.

"Well, between you and me, I think there's something else going on. She can do things that normal people can't."

"What do you mean?"

Doris shook her head. "I don't know. She's really tough on vendors, especially bad caterers. I don't know how she does it, but once you cross her, you're out. No more chances. You'll never work in this town again after Hilde's done with you."

"I heard about that."

"Usually, those guys just lose business and eventually shut themselves down, but sometimes, the vendors just...disappear. No one ever sees them again. It's really weird."

"Yeah."

"We think Hilde belongs to the Mob or a secret society or something. But no one really knows."

We found Hilde waiting for us in front of the mansion, arms crossed and foot tapping.

"Do you like working for her?" I asked, pulling up.

"Ehn. It's a job."

Vases delivered, arranged, and placed, I wandered through the hall with my bridesmaid dress in hand, wondering if Patrick would really call Richard. I wanted to see him and ask him more about his curse, and to be honest, I was kinda craving some high-quality chicken teriyaki.

I found Sam in the bridal suite, giggling and laughing with a few of her friends. She'd already changed into her wedding dress, an ivory satin thing with long sleeves.

"Daisy, did you find Hilde?"

"Yeah."

"Good."

I slipped inside to change into my dress, listening to the girls talk about so-and-so's latest romantic train wreck and whether such-and-such was pregnant or just cutting back on wine.

My ears perked up as Sam said, "Rebecca, you must love San Francisco."

"Oh, it's wonderful. You're going to love it there. It's such a beautiful city."

"I'm sure we will. I just hope we won't be too lonely. It's always hard moving to a new city."

"Don't worry, the people are really friendly. Besides, you guys will have Diego and me."

"I know."

"We'll go out at least once a week. San Francisco has the best restaurants."

Sam sighed. "I can't wait to move. Natalie, I'm so glad you helped me get that interview. Patrick and I are finally going to be together."

"I'm just glad you're joining the firm," Natalie replied. "It's such a great place to work, and they really care about work-life balance. It's much healthier than that other place you were thinking about. I only wish you were staying in Seattle."

"Are you worried about Patrick finding a job?" Rebecca asked.

Sam looked amused. "Patrick is joining Diego's startup. Didn't Diego tell you?"

"Wait, what?"

Uh oh.

"Diego has a startup, right? Patrick told me he was going to join the development team. He's really excited about it. That's the whole reason why we're moving to San Francisco."

I cursed Patrick under my breath. My future brother-in-law was an idiot. As quietly as possible, I inched back toward the door, hoping no one would notice.

"Sam, Diego had a startup, but they lost their funding. He's looking for another job."

"What?!"

"Patrick can't be working at Diego's startup. I mean, Diego was going to hire him, but they lost their funding, and now they're shutting down the company. He didn't tell you?"

There was a brief calm before the storm. Very brief.

"WHERE IS HE?"

One of Hilde's assistants appeared, drawn by the sound of the enraged bride. I made a quick getaway—Sam had enough friends around and I wanted to warn Patrick.

I rushed outside. My heart stopped.

Richard's truck was parked on the other side of the estate, newly washed and sparkling in the murky daylight. I hesitated, then headed toward the truck, only because Patrick was sure to be there, and *not* because I was hoping to see a certain morose, raspy-voiced, long-haired man with bright green eyes.

I spotted Patrick sneaking out a side door and heading for the truck. I hurried faster and cursed my sister for holding her wedding at such a big site. Patrick moved into the bushes, looking around nervously. He'd already changed into his tux and, contrary to earlier claims, it did *not* still fit. He looked ridiculous as he crouched, then scurried to the truck. He took his wallet out and pulled out a card as Richard prepared to hand him a white plastic bag, already prepped.

He really was a glutton sometimes.

Patrick began to hand the card to Richard.

"Last star, huh? What do I get?" he asked.

I gasped.

13

"**P**AT!"
                    I ran as fast as I
could. The men looked up from their transaction.

"Daisy, what's wrong?"

"Don't give him your card," I gasped.

Patrick looked at me like I was crazy, but *he* was the crazy one. I was breathing too hard. "Pat, you can't eat here anymore."

"Why not?"

Patrick already had the bag. Richard gave me a brief, pitying look, then reached to take Patrick's card.

"Well, what's the prize? Free lunch?"

"There's no such thing as a free lunch," Richard replied.

"Patrick." I was almost crying. "You're an idiot."

He looked bewildered, still holding the card. "Why?"

"Because he really is cursed."

"I knew that. He's cursed…with *deliciousness*."

"Dammit, Pat. Don't you get it? Richard's a ghost, and he's about to take your soul!"

"Daisy, what the hell are you talking about?"

"You! I should have known you were here." We turned to see Hilde, nostrils flaring, pigtails blazing behind her. She pointed accusingly at Richard.

The ghost yelped. "You will receive your prize later," he said, then disappeared into the truck.

"Come out, you murderer. I won't let you ruin another wedding." Hilde began to pound on the truck.

Patrick was already halfway through his food. "I need this so bad," he said between mouthfuls.

"Patrick, you idiot," I repeated.

Behind us: "Patrick. You IDIOT."

Sam came blazing fast from nowhere, her dress fluttering behind her. Her pack of bridesmaids surged forward and surrounded the groom.

"I'm not supposed to see you before the wedding," Patrick protested.

"When were you going to tell me about the startup?"

"The startup? Um—"

"You jerk! How am I supposed to trust you? I can't believe you did it. Again."

"I'm sorry, Sam, I was looking for another—"

"I thought we were going to be a team. I thought we were going to tell each other everything. Why didn't you tell me he ran out of funding?"

"Sam, I didn't want you to worry about—"

Hilde stopped pounding. She gave one last glare at the truck, then transferred her attentions to the unhappy couple.

"Stop," she commanded. "Come with me." Hilde's glare stopped the bridesmaids from following as she led Sam and Patrick toward the pond, berating them as they walked.

I looked around. The truck was gone.

It was getting darker outside. Storm clouds were filling the sky.

My parents had missed most of the excitement, occupied with shuttling out-of-town aunts and uncles to the wedding site. Now I stood with them in the alcove waiting to enter the hall, along with Patrick's best man Diego, Patrick's parents, three righteous bridesmaids, three confused groomsmen, two neutral assistants, and one very unhappy (and slightly terrified-looking) couple being guarded by one very large (and slightly terrifying-looking) wedding planner. It was an auspicious start.

Hilde's assistants had herded us up like sheep and we were fifteen minutes ahead of schedule. The guests weren't even seated yet. I peeked through the entryway, admiring Sam's red and silver color scheme hanging velvet along the petal-strewn aisle.

I moved over to talk to Dad.

"How are you feeling?" I whispered. "Happy?"

"Your mom and I are proud that Sam is finally getting married. She deserves to be happy."

Patrick was looking for an escape route. Sam was looking for a weapon.

"I'm glad you're proud of one of us," I said.

"Daisy, we are proud of both of you."

"You can't be proud of me. I'm a terrible daughter."

"You're a wonderful daughter. We just want you to be happy. If school won't make you happy, then we must live with that. You are our daughter first. We will support whatever you decide to do, even if we disagree with your choice."

"Thanks, Dad."

I don't remember much of the ceremony. I get severe stage fright, and it took all my effort to focus on the guy conducting the ceremony without passing out. Someone recited a poem; someone else sang. Patrick read a tender, heartfelt vow; Sam read an angry one. They filled a vase with white and black sand.

Diego reached in his pocket, took out two silk pouches and handed one each to the bride and groom.

The wedding guy stepped forward and clasped their hands. "With these rings, I bind thee—"

Crash of thunder.

"Stop!"

All eyes turned to the back of the room. Richard stood at the end of the aisle, surrounded by a ghostly green nimbus. I felt a sharp pang in my heart.

"You." Hilde's voice rang. "I should have stopped you earlier."

"He is mine."

"No. You shall not take him." Hilde stepped forward into the aisle, her back to the ceremony, eyes blazing, glowing with her own intense red power.

"He is mine by rights. He has been served ten meals ten times from me, and now must he join my blighted crew to serve his own meals to others."

"You shall not take him," Hilde repeated.

"He is mine," insisted the ghost. He pointed at the groom, beckoning slowly.

"Hey!" Patrick tried to resist the magnetic pull. "This wasn't in the contract." He pulled the punch card out of his pocket. "There's nothing on here about eternal damnation."

"Wrong contract," Richard said. Patrick fell forward. The sand vase shattered on the dais.

"I said no." Hilde dug her feet into the ground, shielding Patrick from the phantom. "He will not join your damned crew."

"He's mine!" Sam shrieked, running forward to grab Patrick's leg. "You can't have him."

To my surprise, Mom joined her, undignified, grabbing Patrick's other leg. "Patrick belongs to our family now."

We all rushed toward them then, grabbing, pulling, trying to keep the groom on the stage. Even Great-Aunt Jade lurched forward to help, grabbing at Patrick's head and shoulders. But— the contract was too strong. Our group slid forward, closer, down the aisle as the other guests watched in horror, fled the room, or joined the dogpile.

Richard made a quick motion with his hand. The magnetic pull stopped and everyone fell back. Before we could react, he beckoned again, and Patrick flew down the aisle, landing on his knees.

"I am sorry," Richard said.

Patrick looked up at him, his eyes vacant.

"Wait." I stood up, brushed myself off. Sam had made us pick the most impractical dress, really. This skirt was a trip hazard waiting to happen.

"Don't," Richard said. Pleaded.

"The card's transferrable, right?" I walked forward and plucked it out of Patrick's hand.

"No." The ghost looked horrified. "I tried to protect you."

"I don't need protecting. Let him go. Take me instead. I'll stay with you forever, if I need to."

To my surprise, Hilde spoke up, her intense eyes boring into me. I held steady under her power.

"Do you mean what you say, truly?" she asked.

"I do," I replied. I handed the card to Richard.

There was a thunderclap, then a flash of lighting. The lights went out and the guests began to scream.

Another crash of thunder. The wind began to howl. I heard sounds in it, almost human words—*free, released, saved*.

The lights flickered on a few moments later, full and bright. Outside, the clouds had cleared, leaving an ocean of pale blue sky.

Richard was kneeling on the floor, sobbing; physical, mortal, real. Patrick shook his head as if dazed, looked around, stood up gingerly. He saw the crying figure and put out a hand to comfort him: "Hey, it's all right, man. Everything's okay."

"Patrick!" Sam ran to him, grabbed him, burrowed her face in his chest. He put his arms around her, stroking her hair by habit.

"Sam, what's going on?"

"You're an idiot," she mumbled.

The rest of the evening was pretty uneventful. Somehow, Hilde got the proceedings back on schedule. She glared at the man on the floor and told Doris to get him out of there. The former cursed soul was dragged to his feet and ushered out of the room. I wondered briefly if I would ever see him again.

I did. Later, Richard came to me as I stood outside, breathing fresh air, away from the cacophony of dancing guests. I looked at him in the bright moonlight, patient, waiting.

"Thank you for breaking my curse," he whispered, and leaned over to kiss me.

EPILOGUE

IT WAS SPRINGTIME, March, three months after the wedding. Dad was elbow-deep in tax returns. Mom was helping Sam and Patrick shop for furniture for their new Queen Anne in Queen Anne.

"I'm so glad I'm back in Seattle. It's much more relaxing here. I should have left New York months ago," Sam told me.

Richard's food truck had been destroyed when the curse was broken. To our wonderment, we found a fireproof safe in the ashes, filled with decades and decades of customer payments, a veritable treasure chest of pirate's booty.

With the money, we did what you'd expect—we bought Uematsu House, and I dumped school. It was one thing to be an aimless twenty-four-year-old part-time line cook with no life aspirations. It was quite another to be a twenty-four-year-old full-time entrepreneur with a business plan, a list of recipes, and a lover to whom she was bound through an immortal oath witnessed by two hundred wedding guests. And, a brand new set of charcoals for Christmas. For the first time in my life, I felt like I was living up to my family's expectations.

(Sam's legal opinion was that the immortal oath, being verbally spoken without explicit definition of terms, could not be binding, and that I should be free to leave Richard whenever I liked. I kept that in my back pocket in case the relationship didn't work out, but so far, so good.)

I was glad Sam and Patrick picked Seattle. They'd waffled, but in the end, it was two things: San Francisco's lack of a teriyaki scene, and our business proposition to Patrick—we hired him as our restaurant manager. Having never needed to purchase ingredients or hire employees, Richard had no head for business, and running a restaurant was exactly the kind of challenge to break Patrick out of his career rut.

Sam was a little uneasy about the relationship, partly because she still didn't believe in mixing business with friendship, and partly because of the whole "loss of immortal soul" thing, but Patrick and Richard did know each other from the many meals they'd shared, and the two of them worked well together.

To my surprise, Hilde accepted my request for her to give me art lessons. She swore never to eat at the restaurant, though, and I was disappointed at the missed opportunity for barter.

"That ghost has already poisoned too many with his food," she said, despite my assurance that Richard had learned his lesson about changing people's orders without consultation.

We rounded out the crew with Jay in the kitchen and a few other Uematsu House alumni.

We lost Alice to Spokane, but Jay's daughter was excited about her new job working three afternoons a week in the front of the store. Dad offered to help us with bookkeeping and Mom would also step in until we could hire one or two more people.

"I thought you didn't hire women," I accused Richard one day, remembering. "Men only."

He smiled. "I lied."

Technically, Pat did the hiring anyway.

Our grand opening was in a week. Richard and I stood together in the kitchen, admiring the remodel.

"Candied ginger? That's your secret ingredient?" he asked. The secret had come with the store.

"Yeah," I said. "Grated, so there aren't obvious chunks in the sauce. It takes forever to prep, so we just buy it from a supplier. It's really more of a sweet ginger syrup by the time we're done. What do you put in yours?"

"Soy sauce. Brown sugar. Garlic."

"That's it?"

"Maybe a little honey."

"And ponzu?"

"No ponzu. Lemon peel. Grated."

"Seriously?"

"It adds brightness to the sauce."

"Ha. I want to test the burners. Would you pass me a sieve?"

My ex-phantom boyfriend complied, reaching a long arm into the cabinet above us and handing me a large metal cylinder with holes.

"Lemon peel." I filled the sieve with dry yakisoba noodles and stuck it in a pot of boiling water.

"Yes. And tears."

"What!"

"Just kidding."

"Hmph." I swirled the noodles around. "We're going to have to pick one recipe."

"Or alternate."

"Or sell them as different dishes."

"Or experiment."

"Oh, Jay will love that. He has some great ideas."

Kind of a weird ending, huh? Redemption through love, or maybe just chicken teriyaki. As far as I'm concerned, they're the same thing.

TERIYAKI SAUCE

Recipe by Hisaye and Janis Higaki

1 cup shoyu (regular, not low sodium)
1 tbsp osake
½ cup sugar
1 tsp grated ginger
1 clove garlic, grated

Combine all ingredients and marinate chicken, beef, or tofu for one to two hours. Grill over coals (or on stovetop) until well cooked.

ACKNOWLEDGEMENTS

Thanks to Melissa Edwards and everyone at 3-Day Novel for putting together the coolest writing contest in the world and for giving me such an awesome opportunity. Thanks also to my editor, Kris Rothstein, for her wonderful feedback, support, and patience.

Thanks to Nancy Kress (!), David Figatner, Justin Stamen, Tsu-Yin Chang, Andi Blija, and Jennifer Lin for their additional feedback and advice, and to everyone at Richard Hugo House who commented on the post-contest, pre-win short story version of this manuscript.

Thanks to everyone who gave me slack and support during editing, especially work, the band, the dojo, and kcr who hung out so patiently on zephyr with me.

Thanks to my parents for their support and my family for their inspiration, including all of my cousins who've gotten married in the past two years (and their spouses). I'm sure my subconscious will write my next story about your TBD babies.

Thanks to the Office of Letters and Light and my fellow hydrophobic ducks for re-igniting my writing through NaNoWriMo. I'm glad you exist to challenge slackers like me.

Lastly, thanks to Erica Chung for being the best sister I've ever had (heh), Ben Piazza for giving me space to write, and Brian Perrin for never being a censor. Most of all, thanks to Kei Higaki for the recipe and the motivation—my family's the reason I wrote this book, but you're the reason I wrote anything at all.

ABOUT THE AUTHOR

Jennifer K. Chung is a Taiwanese-American software engineer, writer, and pianist who lives near Seattle. She grew up in Southern California and studied computer science at MIT. In her spare time, Jennifer writes, plays keyboards in a goth metal band called Red Queen Theory, and studies the Japanese martial art of Naginata. *Terroryaki!* is her first novel.